POWER HOUSE MEDIA PUBLICATION

To Gemmel
5.27.11

Aw Shucks!
Diary of a Little Diva

By T. Holland

J. Holland

Sis, this could be about you. R U ready to laugh. Thank you. Enjoy!

POWER HOUSE MEDIA PUBLICATION
NEW YORK

POWER HOUSE MEDIA

POWER HOUSE MEDIA PUBLICATION

Power House Media International LLC.

SAN: 8 5 8 – 3 4 8 X

www.phmillc.com

Designed by Power House Media
Written by Tanganyika "T. Holland" Lindner
Art Directions by Andrae Givans

Manufactured by Power House Media International LLC
For information about special discounts for bulk purchases, please contact
Power House Media Int. LLC special sales department:
contactus@phmstudios.com

Printed in USA
FIRST EDITION

Library of Congress Cataloging-in-Publication Data
ISBN 978-0-9840750-4-1

Dedication

This book is dedicated to you, you and yes you too! I especially dedicate this work to the young people who I have had the pleasure to serve as an educator and trainer. This project is my give back to you all for helping me to never give up. Through this experience I have embodied the idea of perseverance.

This book would have been impossible without the love and support of my family and friends who have listened as I have woven tales and edited pages. To my sister, who tirelessly read every version of this book. To my editor, who was careful to give me honest feedback without hurting my feelings. To my love, who shared pillow space with the pages of my work and encouraged me the whole way.

This book is intended for all audiences. You might find a hint of your younger self, your relative, your student or even your own child. Through this read you will definitely know that each of us embarks on a journey to discover our beautiful selves.

Shout out to Wings Academy!

Enjoy the read. Much love.

Aw Shucks !

Little Diva *(English pronunciation: /*
divə/, Italian: [diva] **:** A young lady who is
confident yet not a woman. She is popular
and stylish in dress also considers herself a
fashionista. Creativity is their anthem and is
reflected in their makeup and hair styles. She
is also intelligent but not arrogant. She is
hated and sometimes envied.

My Mother

She gets on my nerves! She is the root of all evil and the only person that could make me spit such an endearing word like it is poison. She is my mother. She is the woman who stole Pops' heart and conspired to create me many years ago. She is the woman that is biologically responsible for me, well at least half of my DNA. The whole world knows I love me some Pops and everything about him. My mom, there is little except a daily reminder of her existence in the photo on my nightstand. She is this thing, this obviously wonderous thing that was beautiful, strong and most importantly, smart enough to snag Pops. The only reason I do not entertain slapping her (in my mind of course, I ain't no fool) is because of the silly grin on Pops' face in the nightstand photo. Pops gave me this picture a long time ago. He said it was to remind me of who I belonged to and to always know that I was created in love. I remember crying tears of joy when he gave it to me. I used it at my first show and tell presentation in second grade.

Pops' must love her as much as he loves Paul

and I, but I just don't see it. There is evidence of love between Pops, Paul and I wherever you look; it's in our laughter, our greetings, shared meals, outings and photos. Pops knows our friends and even disciplines us when necessary. Of my mother's love, I recall little to nothing.

Dear Diary,

Yes, It's about her again-my mother. How could she possibly love Pops and she is barely here? Usually, by the time I wake in the morning, she is already gone. When I return, she is still not at home. Sometimes she checks on us at night. I can feel her looming in the doorway letting in the bright light from the hall lamp that always interrupts my sleep. I pretend to be off in dreamland. If I were to really wake up what would I say to her, this stranger, my mother? ☺

Diary of a Little Diva

Aw Shucks !

In the 5x7 nightstand photo, she and Daddy are holding hands. There is one hand on her hip and she appears confident. Daddy is looking like a school boy in love. In the picture, his gaze on mother is so direct and full of, I guess, joy that he seems hypnotized. My mother, Zena, is five feet six inches in stature and one continuous piece of raw silk. Raw silk has the audacity to be vibrant and exotic. Knowing its history made it very intriguing. To know that only one type of worm spent a lifetime weaving a distinct pattern to create a silken garment. It was only befitting that my mother would be like raw silk. Mommy had this allure that invited you in.

Her complexion is like warm brown maple syrup over light fluffy buttermilk pancakes. Her legs are strong from her expansive calves that stretch out from her pewter pumps. I imagine that she had a catwalk stride, it not only helped to expedite her travels but to quickly navigate the ladder of success. Which she preferred to walk rather than across our berber carpeted rooms.

In the picture, mother is adorned in a navy blue pinstripe suit. It was classic and professional. The jacket to her suit was open and revealed a lace camisole the exact color of her shoes. Just above the lace in the camisole was

the amplified version of the chest I wish I had.
Knowing my mother she might have gotten some nip
and tuck work done to get her rack, but who would ever
know. I never see her. Even with all the love Pops' and
Paul give me, I still can't stand her. Love over sticky
notes do not count.

Tweet: This is not an office. I am your daughter
and this is real life.

It's a damn shame that the woman at the
make-up counter and Lil Mama's video are the sources
that helped me get my lips kissable. That just ain't
right. Of all the things my mother has including a
loving husband, children and a career, why did she also
have to have a chest?

Triple "A"

Boob development update: It was July 17th and I finally had a glimmer of hope. At the family BBQ at Crotona Park, I overheard my cousin ask,

"Who's that?"

Mike said, "That's Shan, Paul's little sister."

When K responded, "word", I knew something was up.

Then he said, "I didn't know that was family, look at that cake and that shirt is filling out nice."

When I overheard that I was mortified. I just wanted to fall out and die. I couldn't help but think, Is my cousin a pervert?! Am I going to end up on Oprah because my cousin abused me or will I be unable to have a boyfriend because my head is all messed up? My thoughts were stopped before I would allow the drama to proceed any further. I thought to myself, Self, hold up... Didn't he say something about my shirt filling out? Had my kernels started popping? Aw shucks!

Before I could roll my eyes, slap his face or even before Mike could explain what happened, I was jetting across the park to the nearest bathroom. I had to check out the progress of my boob development. Did I wear my push-up or water bra today? I could not remember. Within four minutes I had joined the long bathroom line of a dozen or so women waiting. Some were patient and others were anxious. Some were even engaged in renditions of the pee-pee dance. I didn't care what these women were doing. I had to check the boob development progress. I was pissed, pardon the pun, to have to wait on line another eight minutes. I knew good and well that some chicks were just in the bathroom to gossip, fix their hair, or talk on their cell phones. Why won't these women hurry up.

Finally, I'm next and the girl who comes out of the stall before me announces that there is no toilet paper. I don't care; I just hurry in behind her. I am sure now, people are thinking that I am nasty. They don't know the urgency that required my track star like trot to the bathroom and into the stall. Just for the heck of it, I recall my mantra *a la* Judy Bloom with my eyes closed. "I must, I must, I must increase my bust." Then just before I raise my shirt only to discover I had not worn my water bra, push-up bra, sports bra or any other boob enhancement. I gasp in both surprise and delight.

Diary of a Little Diva

Aw Shucks !

Thanks to my Cousin K, The Pervert, I realized my popcorn was poppin!

In June, before the enlightening BBQ, I had securely put away my 8th grade prom dress and I was ready for all things high school. I planned to spend the larger part of my pre-high school summer walking around in 1.5 inch heels, applying lip gloss and watching music videos. Then I would flip through fashion magazines.

I decided that in high school, I would not be the nervous, naïve, and spoiled little girl that many people thought me to be. I, Shannon Kameron Brown, was no longer Daddy's little girl! I was damn near grown and I was going into high school. There was only one thing missing- A chest!

Despite everything, including workouts, massages and prayer nothing much was happening in the boob area. I am embarrassed to say I adopted Ms. Bloom's mantra, "I must, I must, I must increase my bust" as my own. This lack of boobs determined how I would spend the rest of my summer. No tech camp, summer enrichment or vacationing with family, I was engaged in warfare through my own specially designed

Aw Shucks !

boot camp a.k.a. Boob Development. I spent precious day and evening hours for at least 30 days of summer wondering when I would get some boobs.

I was about to start high school with a chest that looked like a damn triple A battery! I couldn't believe that this was happening to me. All around me chicks were looking like video vixens and Playboy Bunnies. I looked like two popcorn kernels had gotten stuck to my chest. Does anyone besides me know that this was serious.

With another couple of weeks before school began, I still had a chance of getting out of the triple A battery section of life. My Aunt T and other Aunts would say that I was on, "The Itty Bitty Titty Committee." Under my breath I would mutter that they were on the "Saggy, Baggy, Haggie so don't braggie Committee!" I know it's corny, but whenever I say it I feel vindicated. If they could only see me now... Even they would have to admit that I am a dime. Things were beginning to look up, especially since my discovery courtesy of my Cousin K the Pervert. Before I knew it, I would no longer be shopping for Triple A batteries. Would someone say two "C's" please?

Diary of a Little Diva

Welcome to Dimeville

It was summer and I dreamed of being a dime. This of course involved the attention of high school boys that I craved. A dime was considered a 10 on every scale from head to toe. I will do a self-evaluation using the dime scale to prove to you and myself that I was worthy of Dimeville. I had a chance since the standards of beauty had evolved from the 80's where the light skin and long hair no longer guaranteed one a spot in Dimeville, this is the place where all dimes lived. Now a female could be any shade of brown, beige, tan, butter pecan or any spectrum of the rainbow. She could also have various lengths of hair such as Halle Berry or Keisha Cole short, a Megan Good weave or all types of hype like Mary J. Blige. A female could even go blonde and look good, but I digress. Let's go back to my dreams of a being a dime.

On the dime scale, going from head to shoulders for a total of four, I was at least a three. I ranked at least a three, just based on my secret weapon of accessories. They kept all eyes on the face area, to the point just before my invisible cleavage. One couldn't help but notice my accessories. Sometimes I sported 80's style with the old school rope chain, big hoop earrings or the name chain. When it came to accessories you had to know when to wear the bling-bling and when to wear your Mama's pearls. Other days I would wear the big round beads in Skittles or Starburst colors depending on my footwear. If one was going to be a dime contender, your shoe game had to be tight. That meant fly, hip, or just plain fabulous! Shoes were just as important as the outfit and many times the shoes made the outfit. In this area, I wanted to attract the boys, not look like one. So even though I had too many pairs of Timberlands I also wore sneakers and ballet shoes. I was beginning to warm up to Uggz even though they did nothing to elevate me to my desired height of 5' 3". What is the appeal of flat sheepskin boots? I just didn't get it. I could see why guys would call the boots "uglies."

Back to the dime scale. I was already a three and we hadn't even gotten to my lower body. My waist was small and tight. It was accented by Lo Rise jeans that were the perfect style for my pretty brown round. I trust you all know what that is, but in case someone like Aunt T picks this up, I'll break it down for the old heads.

Pretty brown round (n) Any ideas yet? A females butt! Synonyms a phatty or cake. *Ex. That girl's pretty brown round looks proper in them jeans.*

So like I was saying, I always wear oversized belts to emphasize my waist and my cake. What would a dime be without a cake? I can't even imagine. Actually I can imagine, she would be a damn seven that's what she would be! The only thing that was missing from my true ranking as a dime was a chest, which reduced me to a mere 8.5.

I know the movies always show the flat-chested girls stuffing tissues in their bras. With my luck, I would forget the tissues were there and pull one out to blow my nose. Or I would spill water from the fountain and end up with only one boob. Worse than that a cute guy would walk up to me and one boob would fall out. I would just die! Heaven forbid I needed CPR, not only would my disguise be exposed, but my boney chest would probably sink. Thank goodness for my pretty brown round or my cake if you are still following me. I know I'm making you hungry and that's exactly how I wanted the high school boys - hungry. Well, not all of them, but just a few cute ones; maybe even one that was smart.

I felt pretty safe in thinking that I was at least an eight out of ten on the dime scale. This was confirmed by my brother. According to Paul, no matter what your shade of complexion or hair color and even length, a chick was a dime if she was pretty in the face and slim in the waist. At least I had that covered.

Paul was a trustworthy guy when it came to the ladies. I would listen in on his calls or pretend to be busy just near enough to hear him on the phone. He was so slick in how he called all of his females Boo or Baby and they would all just coo and laugh. I thought to myself they were idiots, but I was just hating and wanting that attention myself. When Paul was chatting with those females, I just knew they all had so much more chest than me.

Considering I am only 14 years old, entering high school, an honor student and I have a pretty brown round: I knew I was not starting off bad. Dimeville would benefit by my membership.

Summer School

In high school I heard you have to roll with a crew. You had to have "peoples," especially upper-classmen and co-signers to make you legitimate. I don't know how I feel about that. I was gonna do my own thing. I had no choice. Lea, my BFF (best friend forever) up and moved to some corny assed place of which I can't even remember the name. Oh Yeah... Reston, Virginia, that's why I can't remember. Have you ever heard of Reston?

Her mother, Marcia, is the worse. Just because she met some cute guy who was willing to marry her and make all of her dreams come true, did she have to take my friend away. Lea's mom was like a second mother to me and insisted I call her Aunt Marcia because of this connection. Lea could have stayed with her Dad, even though her parents were divorced. Obviously her mom wanted to start a new life, so they moved and now my life sucks. Thanks a lot Aunt Marcia!

Despite our tears and promises of staying

connected as BFF's, not one email, letter or telephone
call was received or sent. How was I gonna get through
high school? For the last eight years Lea and I have
been to the first day of school together; we shopped
for our clothes together, coordinated outfits and even
walked to and from school together. Who was going
to confirm that I was fabulous or tell me that my outfit
was not fashionable enough? The worst part is that we
had been so tight that there was never much room to let
anyone else in our circle. Besides, Paul was always so
overprotective; He wouldn't even let me get a pet and
we are not even going to talk about Pops.

I was already feeling the pressure of high school
and I hadn't even started yet. With one look in the
mirror I said my own mantra (courtesy of the Pussycat
Dolls), Don't you wish your classmate was hot like me,
Don't cha?

High off my own laughter, I realized every smart
young lady always has to have a Plan B right? So you
know this girl was up all night thinking of how cool I
was, but also of how lonely I would be in high school
so I devised a scheme. Your friend is gone: Do you cry

or meet other people? I obviously decided on the latter.
To increase my chances of meeting people, I
opted to attend the summer freshman program, Building
Bridges. The purpose of this program was to build our
confidence towards success. The program bridged the
learning and social dynamics between middle school and
high school. I know it sounds crazy that someone would
volunteer to go to summer school, but I had. This was
my choice. The one thing I am not scared to admit is that
I have academic skills.

Tweet: The kid is sharp when it comes to school.
Math is not really my thing but I still get B's, I straight
rock honors in Science, and English is my favorite.
Not to brag but, I can converse with the best of them. I
am also a skilled writer with a fierce pen flow.

I had my whole plan figured out. I would go
to summer school to learn and mingle. Now that my
mind was made up, I had only to convince my Dad. He
knows something is going on with me, but he can't figure
it out. Pops knows I'm not doing drugs or having sex,

but he is seeing his little girl growing up. He is so scared that lately he's acting really weird. When I walk in a room he walks out. If I am in the mirror putting on make-up he asks me something silly like, "Where is the remote?" and he has it in his hand. We are not even going to talk about the shorts I wear that make him so nervous he coughs, "Aren't you cold?" I know I am giving him a heart attack, but I am young. I just assure Pops, "Nah, I'm good." He knows something is up because he knows I am never nervous, especially not about school. He just can't figure me out. He blames it all on hormones and cell phones.

Poor thing, that's my Pops. Or maybe it was poor me. I explained to Pops that I was just a little uneasy about starting high school so the Building Bridges Program would go a long way to helping me adjust to the high school beast. My brother even fell for it chiming in, "Yeah school would be good for Shan." What he really wanted to say was that if Shannon is in school that gives me more time with the ladies. Paul is alright, but he thinks he is soooooo cute. He better recognize that his sister is headed to Dimeville.

I was stalking the mailbox waiting for the letter to tell me when my two week program would begin. Between waiting for the letter and tripping on my Cousin K the Pervert who noticed my development, I was going crazy. I began to wonder who else would notice my boob development.

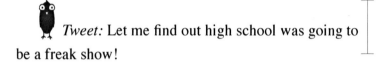 *Tweet:* Let me find out high school was going to be a freak show!

My fantasy world was interrupted with the beckoning of Pops' voice calling my full name, "Shannon Kameron Brown." I could not tell from his tone if the reason he was calling my name was good or bad. Pops was holding a piece of paper, "What did it say?" I ran through my memory bank to see if I was due to get into trouble; room clean, check; dishes put away, check; no grades because it was summer, check; and I know I always presented like a lady; check, check, check. I knew I was cool, so I was confident when I asked, "What's up Pops?" Then I knew it was something great when his face lit up like it did at graduation and he called my name again, "Shan Kam." That's what Daddy calls me.

"Daddy... Just tell me what it is already", I squealed.

I started asking questions quicker than he could answer. "Is it good news? Did we win some money? Is Paul moving out?"

"Shh girl," he said. Let me read the thing. "You Shannon Kameron Brown will attend the SFU's Building Bridges Program in ten days!"

Aw shucks! When Pops told me the great news my thoughts were all over and my questions were many. "When do I begin? At what time? For real? I did it!"

Pops and I danced around doing our silly thing like we did when we were happy. If somebody were peeking through our window, they would think we were a bunch of weirdos but I didn't care. I was glad to have my father sharing this moment.

I was beyond happy to be getting out of the house and for the chance to meet new people. The neighborhood was dead with my friend, Lea, MIA (missing in action). Between Pops and Paul, my teenage life was always closely supervised. The Building Bridges Program made me feel like I was especially selected to be a runway model or a special guest on MTV. Who would have thought that summer school would be a liberating experience? I couldn't wait!

Dear Diary,
August 5th

Daddy and I do our traditional back-to-school IHOP breakfast. (Yes even though it's summer school.) I feel nervous when I am dropped at the doors of Striving for Understanding (SFU), that's my new high school. "Wait, wait", I shouted as Pops attempted to drop me at the front door like I'm a kid. Pops, just leave me down the block; I'll walk the rest of the way. I assure him," Pops, it will be okay. I'll tell you all about it when I get home." His brilliant smile helps both of us feel better. As I take those first steps

Diary of a Little Diva

toward the rest of my life, I say a quick prayer.

God, Please don't let me trip as I walk along this way,

Please don't let me be gassy and have to fart at any time of day

But most of all, let me receive my learning like it is an art

Cuz you know I am cute and also smart. Amen ☺

I giggle aloud remembering that this was me and Lea's thing, but now I entered this phase in my life alone. I don't look back when Pops drops me off because I think I might cry. The last thing I need is for people to think that I am a baby. With my chest poked out, but not too much, I was eager to find out who Shan, the young lady was going to be.

Diary of a Little Diva

My Daddy

Pops has always been patient and smooth. His patience is obvious because the ladies in his life, that is, mother and I. We could drive a saint crazy. Sometimes I think Pops is a sucka. In a traditional relationship, he is definitely the chick. It is he that sees us off to our first days and meets our teachers. Sometimes Moms makes an appearance and then rushes off just as quickly. Pops fixes meals and even cleans house. Now this is not what makes him a sucka. This makes him a responsible man. Daddy is a sucka because I know he loves my mom but he never gets any alone/adult time with her.

My parents' bedroom does not help with setting the stage for romance. Their room is cozy but Mom's side of the bed is littered with boxes and notes from work. She works downtown somewhere. I think she is a legal advocate. Mother is supposedly big business. She is very respected in her field. The mention of the name Zena Brown commands attention.

Given the ice castle of their bedroom, it's a wonder Paul and I ever got made. I guess we were Pops' consolation prizes, so Mom could get back to work.

The notion of Pops being a sucka was forever removed from my thinking on their 20th wedding anniversary. I will never forget this day. This was one of the first times in my school-aged life that Pops was not home for us. He left a satisfactory note on a sheet of paper explaining that he would see us later that afternoon. Thank goodness he did not use a sticky note. His only request was that we come home promptly and tidy up the house. We were glad to oblige.

At 3:45 p.m. into our house entered this man that walked and talked like my Daddy, but this man looked like Adonis. From a fresh hair cut to polished shoes Pops was handsomely dressed. I noticed his manicured hands when he adjusted the cufflinks on his pressed shirt.

Nervously daddy asked, "Do I look I okay?" I was shocked.

I told Daddy, "No, you don't look okay, you look fine..." His laughter helped him relax.

"I'm going to get my lady and celebrate our love" Daddy commented with his chest poked out. "Believe it or not before there was ever a Paul or Shannon there was a Aaron and Zena."

I was in shock. Pops was stepping his game up, being bold even. The spark in his eyes and the stride in his step let me know that Pops was not at all what I had thought. Daddy was just a man very much in love with his wife.

I hope one day to be as fortunate as my Dad. The look on his face was priceless. This memory of Dad's joy stayed with me all day until much later that night. As I settled in to go to sleep, I glanced at the photo of my parents on the nightstand, as I do each night. This was the first time that I had recognized the look on Daddy's face, I had seen it earlier. The look that I saw was joy.

That night I remember the tunes of Stevie Wonder and Marvin Gaye filling the house. I was pretty sure that my parents were making love into the morning. I knew it was a great night because Mommy prepared her famous heart shaped pancakes like she only did during the holidays. She and Daddy were even playing footsie under the table. Paul drove me to school that morning and we joked saying that our parents needed to get a room.

SFU

Walking through those SFU doors for the first time was like being born. Greedily, I took in the scent of the corridors like it was oxygen. The excitement made my heart race until it created its own beat.

I was so distracted by the music of my heart, I barely heard the school safety agent say, "Let me see your ID."

I flashed my lip gloss smile and said, "I'm beginning the Freshman Program, I ain't got no ID."

Way to go Shan, wow them all with your ignorance. I don't think the agent heard me because he asked again to see my ID.

This time, I answered like myself, "I don't have an ID yet. I'm starting the Building Bridges Program today." Thankfully, with a hint of a smile, the comment that followed told me to sit in the cafeteria straight ahead and that I would soon be received by Ms. Linda.

Within five minutes Ms. Linda arrived. It took her an additional five minutes, which seemed like an eternity to her waiting audience. She already had a fan base from the numerous greetings she got from students already attending SFU.

"What up Ms. L?"

"How was your summer?"

"How come you didn't accept me as a friend on Facebook?"

One dude even threw up his fingers to create an "L" and said "L for love." How corny.

Ms. Linda warmly greeted the students and even she had to chuckle. She didn't at all seem like she was some stuck up, frustrated, boring over the hill teacher. She seemed cool. She was so fondly regarded that everyone called Ms. Linda, Ms. L. I quickly decided that Ms. L (I would call her that too) would be one of my allies in this high school experience.

Ms. L began her welcome speech by saying, "Hello, beautiful people.

This little stick of dynamite was draped in a charcoal grey skirt suit and a buttery yellow blouse. Her stockings perfectly matched her complexion so she appeared to have a nude leg and her shoe game was tight. I would definitely have to do a search on-line to find those shoes. They were textured to add dimension to the outfit and were coordinated in the same shade of grey and yellow on her clothes. I swear, she is trying to suck us all in with her charm and presence. I was captivated.

She was probably a dime back in the day.

For myself and those new to the school, we hesitated after taking Ms. L in. We eventually responded, "Good morning" to her "Hello beautiful people."

Ms. L continued her speech, "Welcome to Striving for Understanding, affectionately called SFU. This will now be your home away from home for four years of high school. It will be a fond memory for some, many years beyond. Within these walls and halls, you will meet every life challenge. You will grow into young men and women as you aspire toward a prompt high school graduation. Many people will be there to support you along the way."

She then instructed us to quickly look to our left and our right. "Some of the people you glimpsed will become your friends, college roommates or even business partners. Right now at this very moment, you have to make the important decision about whom and what you will become. That being said, let us begin to build bridges."

She continued by giving us the logistics of the program. We would attend classes on campus for two weeks where we would receive instruction in four basic areas: English, math, science and social studies. As Ms. Linda called our names, we walked forward to receive a syllabus with the names of our advisors. I think her face lit up when she talked about the advisors. "I will introduce you to my esteemed colleagues who will give you a school tour and direct you through your course of study. Any questions?" Ms. Linda seemed cool, but you also got the impression that she was not to be played with. She was barely five feet and everyone seemed to tower over her. I knew that I didn't have any questions.

As instructed, I looked to my left and right. Actually I looked all around me. I was taking in so many bits of eye candy I thought I would go into sugar shock. Needless to say I kept my cool, but I did spot some potential BFF's. From my initial glance I spotted about

Aw Shucks !

four dudes and maybe one female that I might be able
to be friendly with.

When I followed my advisor Ms. McKay, I
noticed only one of the guys I had spotted earlier. The
female that was with him would now be in my group. I
was quick to extend my hand and immediately whipped
out my street lingo. "What's up? The name is Shan."
Could you believe that dude barely gave me a nod? I
thought he was checking me out? Thought to self:
Don't try that crap again.

I had to admit I was pissed that dude played me.
I was not to be ignored. I could not believe he was
acting brand new. Did he not see me? I know I am a
lot of things, but invisible I am not. When I walk into a
room I leave a lasting impression. Or at least I had until
now. He wanted me, who was he kidding? Okay, so
maybe I am getting carried away, but he didn't have to
ignore me.

The First Day

I was over the newness of SFU. The Building Bridges program had provided the perfect orientation. I knew where most of my classes were and had an ally in Ms. L. You best believe that the cutie that ignored me earlier would definitely become my friend. I also hoped to find the female from summer that seemed cool.

I really missed Lea when it came to wardrobe issues like the first day. She was such a fashionista. We were like Puff and Biggie. I am the brains and she is the talent and charm. With Lea's input, I would have been sure to be the envy of any student freshmen or upper-classmen. It was friggin' pissing me off that she was not here!

After much anguish and a destroyed room, I decided on skinny jeans, a bright Aeropostale shirt in hot pink with a believable water bra and wedge sandals for the first day of school. Despite my petite frame, I wore wedges because I wanted my inner confidence to be matched by my height. Standing at what I considered an elegant 5 feet 4 inches, it was official I was in high school.

Aw Shucks !

Dad still insisted on driving me to school but the same rules applied as they had during the summer, he would drop me off down the block. In a weird rescue mission Paul offered to drive me instead. Thank goodness. He even complimented my outfit. I was so waiting for my membership into Dimesville. Paul's compliment was like a letter of recommendation.

This actual first day experience was so much different than my summer entry when only a few folks were sprinkled in a few hot spots in the school. Most of the students who attended in the summer were either new admits, accelerated students and those who were trying to avoid the five year high school plan. Today it was crowded with students and many new faces. Suffice it to say, I could already spot a junior from a senior. I mostly recognized freshman or fresh-meat as I soon learned incoming 9th graders were called because of how they looked confused about where to go.

Eagerly I searched for a friendly face even if it was that cornball Corey. This was the guy who had not acknowledged me during the summer. This was also the guy who had a secret crush on me. It was such a secret that even he wasn't aware.

Aw Shucks !

With all the confidence I could muster I did my best imitation of what I had seen other students display when they saw Ms. Linda and I said, "What's up Ms. L ?" with a beaming smile. Ms. L responded with an enthusiastic wave and a, "Hello Shannon."

It was not until nearly the end of the day that I saw a familiar face. It was the female from summer, but I couldn't remember her name to save my life. She sure did know who I was. She waved frantically like a grandmother in the airport. I was almost embarrassed for her and wondered if I had looked like this when I greeted Ms. L earlier. Yikes. I hope not.

"Hi "

"Hey girl!" I responded to the air when I realized the wave was not intended for me.

The conversation that I witnessed continued with, "How was the rest of your summer?" Mine was cool. I went to Florida, I responded in my head.

Surprisingly, Nikki, had a lot to say for a girl. I learned her name when her friend said goodbye as they parted to their separate classes. I had a good feeling about Nikki. She seemed cool. Then out of nowhere we heard a male voice echoing, "Word!" Both Nikki and I turned our heads to follow the voice of the word spoken to find Corey on the other end. You know I am tight now, what does he want, other than me?

Tight (v)- A feeling of anger.
Ex. I know you were tight when you could not go to the dance last week.

As I walk towards my homeroom, I find Nikki in enough proximity to start a real conversation.

"Hi, I'm Shannon."

Nikki laughed, "Yeah I saw you trying to say hello earlier. I'm Dominique but everyone calls me Nikki."

With that quick introduction she walked into her homeroom which was across the hall from mine. Again I pretended as if we were friends already and shouted,

"Okay girl; Talk to you later," I shouted.

I left cute Corey standing there by himself. If Dominique and Corey were trying to ignore me, I could ignore them too.

Aw Shucks !

Before I could tease Mr. Corey anymore, the bell rang to end homeroom. At the same time noticed the whole tone of the hallways changed. I literally watched heads turn.

"Shhh…," Corey said.

Our eyes followed the scene. In silence we struggled for words to connect to what was happening right before our eyes. What we did not realize is that we had been given an audio cue that signaled the meeting of a school icon and someone who would definitely cover many pages in the year book.

Ms. Thang

The click clack of her heels made a melody against the linoleum tiles. The syncopation of her heels let you know that she walked with confidence. This was not the stride of an administrator or the stomp of an irate parent coming to collect their child. This was the walk that said, "I know I am Naomi Campbell, Look out Tyra, I am America's Next Top Model!"

The click clack was a recognized sound like a child's cry or the distinct way your mother calls your full government name to get a certain response. Click clack click clack began the sound track of this high school adventure. It was Nia that would become infamous by this sound.

It happened every 50 to 53 minutes, the sound that lulled you, irritated you. The sound made girls jealous and want to send text messages of love to their boyfriends. Some even ventured to imitate the walk that commanded attention. If P Diddy was at our school, he would remix that sound and Nia would be making the friggin' band. Aw Shucks!

Aw Shucks !

The one woman band was Nia. Nia, was not short or tall and certainly not average. God no, anything but that. Rightfully, she would have to be called petite and this might be the only way you could ever put her in a category even remotely related to small was when it came to her height. Let's be clear, Nia was petite. Be assured that even in her stature, absolutely NOTHING was lacking in her person. And if for some crazy reason you would ever dare to forget the click clack of the short stack that was Nia, she would haunt you. I had heard that Nia was like a firecracker with a short fuse and ready to explode. Her click clack was like the timer on a bomb. I didn't want to be there for the fireworks.

The sound went "click clack click clack click clack." It signaled it was September and Nia was back.

Lonely Girl

High school was proving to be quite wack. Every afternoon, when Pops asked about my day, I had to stretch to come up with an interesting imaginary scenario. One that spoke about all that I was learning. Truth is, I was feeling quite lonely. I had no friends.

There are visions in my mind when I am cool with Nikki and Cute Corey, but my mind is as far as the connection goes. There were no phone calls, emails and definitely no hanging out stories. While I had actually exchanged brief words with Dominique and Corey most of the encounters I initiated. The only evidence of my remotely knowing anyone at SFU was through fabricated Twitter conversations. Anyway you sliced it, high school suuuuccckkeddd if you were not confident. What would become of my high school journey? Would I ever get a friend or a B-cup? My head was already full and now I have to face lunch.

The lunch time bell was like a death knell. It was the sound to which most young people flocked. It could be viewed as a liberty bell; liberty from the classroom rule restrictions, academia, and especially teachers. Lunchrooms gave way to relaxed posture, casual language and the many possibilities of mayhem. "Ah," was the sigh of most. "Yippee," was the joy of others. Giggles escaped the pouty mouths of girls who could not find words as they saw cute boys pass. I was in neither of these groups. For me lunch time was a death knell and I marched toward the cafeteria doors like a pallbearer. I lamented this hour as evidenced by my bowed head and averted eyes. "Oh my gosh," my soul cried, What am I going to do now?!

Like a trained dog, I followed the person in front of me. Four steps. Turn right. Then like the person before me, I collected a tray, I scanned the edible options or at least I thought they were edible. The chicken surprise concerned me. I followed the leader so salad and french fries became my lunch too. I was so transfixed on following the person before me that I nearly followed her to a table that was obviously full except for the reserved seat for my fearless leader. Quickly, I eyed an empty table and boldly sat alone to hastily consume my lunch. After eating approximately eight fries, I was filled with discomfort and decided to exit.

Aw Shucks !

The clock showed only 12:25 p.m. My first official high school lunch room episode lasted less than ten minutes. Already I had bolted for the refuge of the bathroom or the library. The bathroom won out simply because of its closeness. When I arrived at the bathroom, I quickly reasoned that I was not the only girl who thought to bolt. In fact, I was at the end of the line as I held my right foot against the bathroom door to keep it open. The time was now 12:30. Forget this... off to the library. I am sure that I had one of my fancy hair or fashion magazines in my oversized purse.

Now this is what I call lunch.

Playlist

High school requires great navigational skills. Summer school had lulled me into a false sense of comfort. There was this easy pace of movement between classrooms and hallways not littered with people. September's pace was much quicker with people grooving to music that everyone was not cued to. It was like a scene out of a movie. Imagine that you are a casting director looking for new stars for your upcoming film. This is what I am thinking as I walked through the halls of SFU. Who are the major and minor characters? Who would forever be an extra? Freshman, were barely considered extras. I was not at all comfortable with this ranking and aspired to alter my position immediately.

I continued to look for other characters. My eyes were my imaginary video camera. Some of the snapshots my lens captured were brown, white, red and beige complexioned hormonal teenagers in all heights. They had manes from mullets to Mohawks. Some sashayed, ran, jogged and/or strutted through the hall. Some wore a range of styles; from ball gowns and g-strings to designers. They included Aeropostale, Abercrombie & Fitch. Also included were Eddie Bauer, Macy's and Target.

From such a quick glance, you could not easily decipher who was who. Upon closer inspection you could begin to recognize certain groups. It was based on attire, language and handshakes that showed their allegiance. The most obvious group was The Jocks. Some dudes were casually hosting the gun show by displaying their rippled arm muscles. Others showed taut muscular legs and stood strong in much too large basketball shorts. I could not wait for football season to see guys saddled up in their form fitting football attire. Go team! I planned on exhibiting lots of school spirit.

Athletics was not unique to the guys. The ladies represented for teams too. The most notable team was the Dynamic Divas, our step team. They were sponsored by the illustrious women wearing crimson and cream of Delta Sigma Theta Sorority, Inc. They sometimes came for surprise appearances. The presence of these college women even made the jocks drool. These sisters were always prompt, in business attire and respectful. Most importantly they taught girls to step hard. I know stepping is like African boot dancing. I swear the Dynamic Divas were trying to be heard by their sisters in the Motherland!

I cannot forget our other notable team, Hoopstars. The number of banners that hung from the rafters at SFU made the school gymnasium feel like Madison Square Garden. Hoopstars, had titles going back 10 years and our school is only 12 years old. The popularity of the girls' team has grown so much that chicks would transfer mid-year, even senior year, to have their names displayed on the Hoopstars roster.

Hoopstar girls were known as a tight pack. It was difficult to enter their circle if you weren't a serious baller. You qualified as a baller in one of four ways: 1) You were a member of Hoopstars; 2) You played with an outside league comparable to Hoops; 3) You dared to get on the court and could handle your business with a basketball. This third position was probably the most dangerous. If you could hold your own you would definitely get pressed, highly encouraged that is, to link up with a team preferably Hoopstars: you could also be down with this pack of foxes if 4) You were romantically involved. Of course not all female athletes like other females, but some were certainly dating girls, playing tongue hockey or at least admitted to being bi-curious about females.

There is another group of females that put me in the mind of a hip hop classic by LL Cool J, "Around the Way Girl." The lyrics say, "I want a girl with extensions in her hair/ bamboo earrings at least two pair/ A Fendi bag and a bad attitude that's all she needs to get me in a good mood/ She could walk with a strut or talk her street slang, I love it when a woman ain't scared to do her thang (and my favorite part)/ she was standing at the bus stop sucking on a lollipop…"

These lyrics epitomize a girl duly named Lollipop Lisa. LL Cool J must have graduated from SFU because much of what I see walking through the hall is reminiscent of his song lyrics. A Lollipop Lisa is not quite comfortable being a girl, but she can appear as a sexy tomboy. Her pants are extra baggy, her hair is usually off her face and in a ponytail and she wears classic sneakers such as Shelltop Adidas, Stan Smiths or Pumas. Lisa stands much like a dude with her feet shoulder width apart and of course she has a lollipop in her hair. Lollipop Lisa's can hang with the best of them. Lisa can ball with the guys, flirt with the girls or even go solo. For her appearance, she stands out. In all actuality, a Lollipop Lisa is the greatest chameleon.

The freshmen or Fresh-meat group was where I fell in. I was an extra on the side stage of high school. I learned that freshmen had gotten their label-freshmeat honestly. Both males and females became prey for upperclassmen to catch. The scent of new students or meat wafted through the halls and made hungry predators salivate. The chase was quickened by incoming students wanting to belong.

It was in the first year that some students got introduced to gangs, drugs and some students gave away their virginity just for a seat at the lunch table. Some continually donated the bodies or switched allegiance once they realized they were discarded by their conquerers. The only thing that saved me from being a total outcast and looking like a lost puppy was the

Aw Shucks !

Bridges Summer Institute. That's where I was able to learn my way around the school and meet Ms. L. While I was certainly feeling the pang of being a lonely extra, I was a first year high school student. I was nobody's freshmeat.

So far, my gaze has only focused on the obvious groups, mostly teams, but we cannot forget the cultural connections that exist between individuals. There are gays/lesbians, blacks and Latinos, and the solo acts. Just like the Lollipop Lisa's, homosexuals, gays and lesbians, were more readily identifiable by their outward expressions. Sometimes I was thoroughly confused about gender issues. Girls had bass-like masculine voices. Males had shapely asses and wide hips like women. Females that were openly gay often masked the shape of their breasts under a sports bra. It was topped with an A-line t-shirt, most commonly referred to as a "wife beater." Other females were just tomboyish; wearing jeans sneakers and hoodies. Or skirts and sneakers. Openly gay males had a tendency to hang with the creative types; like dancers and actors. Their clothing could be easily mistaken for an art canvas; where they were a one of a kind original. The whole sensation of skinny jeans intended for males sometimes even confused and amused this group because the skinny jean style was open to all and not a way to label any one group. The boys just thought there were more people for their team. Yippee!

Blacks and Latinos were an odd group. Despite integration laws, they still remained very separate, by choice. Sometimes out of fear of the unknown or comfort, we just stick to our own kind. Commonalities among people extend beyond culture and race into neighborhoods and communities. So while black girls range in hues from light bright and damn near white, cream, cocoa, oatmeal, honey, and brown sugar all the way to fudge brownie. A Latina from Cuba, Honduras or Puerto Rico could also be included in a set with black girls if she was from the same neighborhood. Similarly, Latinos are mostly bound by the sweet rolling R of their culture with a side of arroz y gandules or rice and beans. The shades of some of our Latin family range in hues from arroz, dulce de leche, the sticky brown of freshly fried maduros or the brown of "concon" the darkest brown of the bottom of a cooked pot of rice. As individual as each culture is, there are opportunities for blending fried chicken and collard greens with arroz y gandules. A darker skin brother may speak Spanish and a "latin" looking brother "no hablo espanol." Comprende?

Humanity transcends the most basic definition of connection, so no matter how you defined yourself you were free to roam about the halls, walls and buildings of SFU as you saw fit. Some of us just initially identified with the images most close to our own reflection in the mirror.

Finally, the solo acts could be renegades or chameleons that could fit easily into any group but they were perfectly comfortable in their own skin. Solo acts could be seen in any of the aforementioned groups because they were just cool like that. This was the position I coveted most. Maybe this was the ticket. Since Nikki barely wanted to speak and Corey did not want to own up to his desires for me, I certainly was not going to settle for being an extra or a side of fresh meat. Maybe just maybe I would be a solo act. Huhhmmm?

Still Lonely

Monday

After a few weeks of watching high school from the sidelines, I jumped in like a cheerleader at a half-time show. The next day I decided to play it cool, I was not going to be anxious or appear desperate for friends. I would continue to ignore Mr. Corey and that Dominique, because I didn't know what to do with her. Maybe I would just give her the nod of acknowledgment with my chin and not waste my precious words. I would never risk getting embarrassed as I had the first time, when I was waving frantically. Not me, not again. I might even wear some stilettos to see if I could garner the same attention as Ms. Thang. Who was I kidding, I could barely wear a wedge!

This day was a complete loss, but nothing ventured, nothing gained. Tomorrow would be better.

Tuesday

I entered school promptly and began what I

noticed was a routine. Each day I sat in the café sipping my hot tea with lemon. I sat facing the door so I would not miss any action. While sipping my tea, I usually saw Dominique, Corey, I guess, didn't usually arrive at school until later. After my tea was done, I went to my locker pretending to rearrange books. Then I sat in the library.

As the wheels in my head started turning, I felt bold and empowered. I decided to change my routine this very instant. I got up, threw the remainder of my tea away and proceeded to the bathroom. My morning mirror inspection was new. I never expected to find a gaggle of girls primping and changing into skimpier outfits and shorter skirts. I almost had to wait for a spot to apply my lip gloss then I remembered the compact stuffed at the bottom of my bag that I had received from my mother. The compact was wrapped in black satin and had round mirrors on both sides. One was a magnified mirror in case of harsh lighting mother warned. When the compact snapped closed it revealed the perfect red lipstick kiss. After a successful discovery of the compact, I retouched my lip gloss and was ready to exit. Before my expeditious bathroom departure, I was pretty sure that I heard Dominique utter, "Hey." I just gave her a nod by jutting out my chin and exited. I could tell Dominique was salty because she exited close behind me. I made a b-line to my locker, only to discover that a few lockers down was Nikki at her locker.

Salty (v)- A state of being bitter.
Ex. Nikki was salty when I nodded and walked away.

Dominique walked over to my locker in a quick and intentional pace. Was this going to be a fight? Did I have toilet paper on my shoe? A huge zit? Not to be caught off guard, I slammed my locker to signal that I witnessed her approach.

Within two seconds and in a voice of disgust Dominique asked, "What's up?"

I responded coolly, "What's up with what?"

"With you! One day you want to be all chummy and the next day you are as cold as ice" Dominique stated.

I retorted, "Nah, It's not even like that. Day one I waved at you and you just played me. Then later the same day you just brushed me off and that's not going to happen again. If you want to be friendly, be consistent. If not that's cool too. Later."

I don't know where I got the courage to be so bold and sassy. If I kept this up I might never have a friend. Either way, I was glad that I had taken charge and ended the conversation with Dominique this time. I was nervous because I didn't know how my response would go over but I was willing to risk it.

Again I was on the move. I walked away with my chest puffed out.

The day was coming to an end and I was at my locker again. I was almost startled when I closed it to find Dominique on the other side.

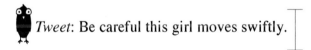 *Tweet*: Be careful this girl moves swiftly.

Wtf? Did this girl want to do me harm or was she extending an olive branch? Cautiously I waited.

She began the conversation in a bubbly voice asking, "Hey what's up?"

"What's up?"

"You don't remember my name do you?"

Diary of a Little Diva

57

Since Dominique was playing nice and blonde I would play along, "I remember your face from the summer, but most unfortunately, I cannot recall your name. My apologies."

With a chuckle she responded, "I'm Dominique, but you can call me Nikki."

"I'm Shannon, but I think you know that"

"Shannon, where are you from, sounding all white and proper"

"I know you didn't just say that because I use proper diction and enunciate words that I'm white. No Boo, It's right!"

"Ok, Shannon, where are you from?" I'm bi-borough. I represent both the Boogie Down and Harlem. What about you?"

"I'm from the Boogie Down, Castle Hill, never ran and never will." Both Nikki and I couldn't help but laugh.

Then Dominique chided, "So you gangsta now Shannon?"

"Whatever!" I responded. Then I asked the essential question, "So Dominique… Are we going to be cool or what?"

"Yeah Shan, we cool."

It was just at this moment that I turned my head to find Corey once again in earshot of our conversation. It was okay because I was enjoying the view.

D$

Everyone has a story right? So why would Dominique dka Nikki be any different.

DKA (n)- Diva known As

Ex. Ms. Linda dka Ms. L, is our advisory teacher.

Like I said from the beginning Dominique had a lot to say for a girl. My experiences with females have been limited. Of course, I have a mother, but I learned about females from my favorite guys, Pops and Paul. I was taught that females should be seen and not heard or pretty in the face slim in the waist. Maybe I was naïve, but I reserved my speaking for something important. Since Nikki was such cool people and one of my only friends at school, who was I to judge. The same way I had ideas about her, she probably had thoughts about me, including that I was weak for not speaking up more. Strange thing is friendships open windows to secrets and begin to reveal the true person beyond their hard or soft exterior. In any case, I was definitely considering Nikki

as BFF potential. Already I liked her style. She was
not overexcited to meet me and even tried to test me at
my locker. Maybe just like I was lonely, Nikki was a
place to belong too.

Nikki began to reveal herself in ways that I had
never expected. Now that I'm thinking about it, I recall
the time me, Nikki and Corey, Oops, Nikki, Corey and
I, went to Mickey D's. Corey and I each had a $5 bill
and one or two singles. Nikki confidently asked if the
establishment accepted credit and gingerly slid her
American Express to cover the purchase of her meal.
Corey and I gave each other the "Okay" look to signal
that was not what either of us had expected, but it was
time to grub so we would let that slide. Secretly we
began to call Dominique, D$.

At other times, I would find Nikki matching
my wit when I told a sarcastic joke or made some slick
remark. I loved when people had mental skill. I'm not
talking about those mind games, but those who are not
scared to flex their mental muscles. I especially dig
those who engage in meaningful dialogue using the
expanse of their lexicon: all while keeping current with

cultural and urban vernacular. Now that's what's up!

I became less caught off guard when Nikki added her commentary to my start and before you knew it we were engaged in lengthy banter about any random topic that would continue via Instant Messaging courtesy of Facebook or Twitter. This was only the beginning of our friendship. Little did I know how crucial this friendship would be to both of our lives.

Corey

IDK, I don't know, what could I say about my boy Corey, except that when I first saw him at the summer orientation something drew me to him. Maybe it was the way he moved. I was drawn to Corey the same way I was drawn to Nikki and Ms. Linda. My spirit just knows good people.

Corey was tall. His complexion the color of dark smooth fudge. He was like a tasty desert that you could only eat in small portions. While everyone thought him yummy, you could tell he was not quite comfortable in his skin. Out of 100 percent for confidence he was at least an 89. Where Corey was not lacking was in the brilliance of his smile. When I think of Corey and his smile, I can only conjure the visual of the old school hip-hop classic, Mona Lisa by Slick Rick. One line says, "When I smiled almost blinded her." But this was me, Shan, talking about my boy, my brother, Corey. He could never be more than aiight. Cute would be pushing it. Admittedly, other chicks swooned, giggled and even cut their eyes at Nikki and I because Corey was our boy. He let it be known proudly. We were so close he almost never used our names or saw us as individuals. We were an entity "His girls".

Corey's parents were married and despite new statistics, this was not a novelty. Many of my friends' parents were married. Some of them even had multiple homes, cars and a picket fence. My address did not define me, last I checked love was still free and no matter your socio-economic background, everyone really just wanted to be loved. This was probably one of the few ways poor and marginalized people closed the gap or even outstretched a hand to grab a hold of the American Dream. Whatever that is. I am off my soapbox now.

Corey always smiled that big goofy smile when he spoke of the folks. That's what he called them, like he was out of some damn movie "My folks this" or "My folks that." I guess it must have only been them, because aside from the folks and his girls, Corey did more listening than talking.

Paul

Talking about my relationship with Corey reminded me of Paul. My big brother is every girls dream; he is a gentleman, attentive, athletic and smart. This is also why all his ladies are my nightmare. I would never want Paul to be hurt or used. If necessary I would kick some ass for my bro.

Paul and Pops are the first examples of love that I have ever known. Paul is only two and half years older than me, but I regard him as a sage. Paul's nickname is Ping Pong. He got his name because of his head. When Paul was born he had a teeny tiny head. When Pops held his first born child, he didn't think Paul, he thought Ping Pong.

Paul would kill me if he knew I shared this with anyone. Even sometimes when we are home alone he cuts his eye at me if I try to call him Ping Pong. Just like me, Paul is close with Pops so if Daddy calls him Ping Pong it is their way of bonding.

Aw Shucks !

My brother and I don't have the typical older brother younger sister relationship. It doesn't annoy Paul to drive me to the mall or give me an opinion on an outfit. Sometimes we hang out or watch a movie just because we enjoy each other's company. It is from Paul that I learned my ABC's and got my love from books.

Paul graduated high school a year early. He is home now just trying to figure out his next steps. Whichever direction he takes, I know he will meet with success. I just hope I am as successful especially if he leaves the house. Life without Paul at home would be a different place.

"Yo Mama!"

Even though I loved and hated my mother. I would never speak of her negatively, especially not in public. I should have been shocked to hear, "Yo Mama," yelled across the hallway, but somehow I expected this of high school students.

"Yo Mama!" These were the most popular and infamous words ever spoken by young mouths. These two simple words could end you up on the other side of life. Sometimes people received it with the humor in which it was intended. At other times, you felt like you were on the set of Hollywood movie horror film, where even as the director you did not know the outcome. People were out of character.

Ms. Linda directed the advisory portion of our learning. Our advisory period was not supposed to be about academics. It was the school's way of getting us to open up through discussion and self-expression as we explored the elusive question, Who am I? Ms. Linda is real personable. I told you I felt connected with her from the beginning. She had an appeal and a swagger that just drew you to her. I guessed that this is what it might feel like to have a relationship with your mother. You related to Ms. L the way you would relate to one of your Aunts that was mad cool. Yeah, she was definitely the Auntie type. When you spoke to Ms. L, you did not feel like you were exposed or vulnerable to stranger. You were rather comforted by this logical, mature, fun-loving, silly adult who you trusted knew just a little bit more about living than you did. Funny thing, Ms. L used this information against you, but not in the classic psychology way. Instead, Ms. L gave your words back to you like a gift when you needed encouragement.

It was no wonder that during one of our advisory self-exploration sessions, Ms. L asked, "Who are the women in your lives?" Only she would ask such a question. The room filled with a cacophony of my moms, mi madre, ma dukes, madear, and mother. I never know how to respond to anything related to my mother. I just looked around the room. I noticed Nia's silence along with my own.

Nia, although almost two years ahead of me was in our class. It was SFU's attempt to mix the dynamics

of non-academic classes to forge mentoring and
supporting relationships amongst students. Anyway,
Nia was not my peeps but we had spoken once or twice.
I would especially notice her silence because I am such
a voyeur. Even when I am fully engaged in action, I am
still surveying the scene. I am sure this is a talent that
has yet to be named. But before I could make a gentle
approach toward Nia, a loud assed ghetto girl wanna be
dime named Tre said, "What up with you Gucci girl,
You don't have no women in your life? You might
be fly, but your life is wack! At least everybody got a
mama even if she get on your nerves. You ain't got a
mama?"

Shaken out of her far off gaze Nia collected
herself like she was before a jury. She looked the
accuser right in the eyes and without any emotion in her
voice Nia simply and calmly stated, "No, I no longer
have a mother. She has transcended this Earth."

In response, the room went pin drop silent.
Even Tre had the good sense to lower her head. I
thought Ms. L was going to slap the crap out of
Tre. This was definitely an "Aw Shucks" moment. I

couldn't help but turn my head in anticipation of what would happen next. The only rule that Ms. Linda had was the following: Always show and have RESPECT. She explained that respect applied to learning, your instructors, the school facilities, all people and especially ourselves. Ms. L was able to get us to recite this rule with just a mere glance: RESPECT.

Just as quickly as the mother bear's gaze changed from defense to one of comfort Ms. L looked at Nia and winked. When Nia winked back, Ms. L redirected her attention and damn near went off. Between her clenched teeth and very narrow, almost Asian eyes, she spat at the class her only rule: RESPECT. I want to ask you all a few questions concerning my only rule,

"Is Tre respecting herself?"

"NO" the class answered.

"The class?"

No."

"Learning?"

"No."

"Personal space? Her instructor? This building?"

The questions came quicker than the class could respond and with each bullet of a question Ms. Linda walked closer to Tre and leaned so close until I thought it was gonna be some freaky-deaky Brittney-Madonna kiss. Her movement was followed by an inaudible utterance. Several minutes later Tre passed Nia a note. They both exited. All the while I could not help but think: This ain't algebra, but x + y could still equal Aw Shucks!

Class wasn't over yet but the silence still lingered in the room. You could hear the wheels of peoples' minds turning as they wondered what Ms. L whispered and what Tre had scribbled in her note. We felt bad for Nia, but didn't want to pity her. We were also mad as hell with Tre, but still had to show respect. We knew this situation would get handled. We just had no idea of how it would unfold.

Even in the thick of this moment, Nia's stride did not change. With the note in hand, the famous click clack walked out of the room followed by an embarrassed, almost humble Tre. I played out the hallway scene in my mind like this: Nia has her arms crossed against her chest looking at Tre smiling with the Tyra eyes look that says, "Yes bitch what you want!" Whatever the exchange was it was quick and almost as quickly as they exited the room the famous stiletto click clack was back. Nia resumed her seat and rightful place in the classroom. Tre did not come back into the room.

There were still ten minutes left to class. There was no way in hay that Ms. L was going to just let us chill, so we all just dug in and continued what we had started talking about- the women in our lives. What followed next was one of the many reasons Ms. L was so fondly regarded.

She too kept the pace of her voice normal as she spoke, "So Nia we did not get a chance to hear about the woman in your life. Who is your shero whether she is here with us or beyond? Do tell."

Nia stated that she had been waiting for this moment, but never knew it would happen like this. Actually, I have two sheroes. One is my Mom. I waited six years after her passing hoping my feet would grow to connect with her. The shoes that most of you hate to hear belonged to her.

Some of my classmates laughed at the mention of Nia's shoes. Nia continued, "My other shero is my

Aunt T. She is the bomb." We were all surprised that she spoke. Imagine if Tre had waited just a few more minutes, Would Nia have mentioned her Aunt? Had she wanted to speak about the mother she lost? Nia might have even shared that in a different way. I guess we will never know.

Once again, the room seemed light and cool just the way you expected it to be in Ms. Linda's class. This was also the day I decided to add Nia to my roster of people. There were only two people on the list, but they both mattered. I wondered if Nikki and Corey knew Nia beyond the first day of school when her shoes were causing a distraction. To keep things moving in the right direction, I shouted for Nia to hit me up on later, my screen name is "Sweet n lo 10."

Nia stood quietly for a minute either trying to figure out what I was asking her or my screen name. To help resolve the confusion, I asked, "Gucci Girl, You gonna make me break it down? You know from experiencing class with me, that I'm sweet. My height is obviously the lo, and you know I'm 9 cents on the dime scale so I just rounded up to 10. So like I said hit me up at sweet n lo 10, alright Gucci Girl? You know what I'm going to call you GG, short for Gucci Girl. Tre had that right; you got a little flavor.

GG had the nerve to respond, "I'll give you an 8 on the dime scale."

"Whatever." I responded.

GG laughed a hearty laugh and promised to hit me up later.

Before I was too far gone I hollered, "GG?"

"Yeah."

"Sorry about your Moms. I always knew it was something special about them shoes."

"Thanks Shannon."

"Aiight"

"One."

Aiight (v) an abbreviation of alright that signals agreement or state of being   good. *Ex. How you feeling? I'm aiight.*

One (n)- closure. Usually a way to end a conversation, synonymous with okay, or to   show unity as in one mind. *Ex. I will talk to you later, one.*

Angel

Dear Diary,

When your mother is dead and people
know, it changes the playing field. Like
when you get into a verbal exchange with
someone, it always leads to the inevitable
"your mother" and then the person
remembers your mother is dead. An
argument that should result in the
opening of a can of whip ass because a
person dared to engage in verbal warfare
suddenly becomes squelched with a
pathetic, "I'm sorry." Fortunately, for
my opponent I accept and have to
gracefully bow out. May is especially the
worst time of year where debutantes are
entering cotillions, mother and daughter
teas and of course Mother's Day. I can
hear the sighing of onlookers, " Aw, she
has no mother." This makes me so
angry-their pity. At these points I can

see me crushing them with my bare hands. It is they that I wish to be six feet under in a pile of dirt instead of my mother, my angel.

I can't believe that I revealed my secret! I still can't believe that when Ms. L asked about women in our lives, I didn't immediately talk about Aunt T. Even more shocking was the calm when Tre said, " Ain't you got no mother?" Not only was it ignorant, it was grammatically incorrect to boot, damn trick. Once again, I'm getting off track from the fact that I announced to a room of strangers and haters that the most beautiful soul I have ever known was dead, she no longer exists on Earth! The way I said it almost cheapens who my mother was and makes it seems like she didn't leave her legacy pumping through my veins.

Even now my head fills with hundreds of memories thinking of my mother, Ms. Lynn Jacqui Richardson. Aunt T says the boys used to say Ma was like hot chocolate, you had to hold her with both hands

Diary of a Little Diva

and even then you could only indulge in sips. Aunt T
said the only drug my Dad ever did was my Mama.

Despite a very tattered picture mostly pieced
together by Aunt T, I know my mother was a dime. Her
smooth complexion was the color of toasted almond
that you were eager to get from the ice cream truck.
Her dark eyes were placed in her face at a slant,
surrounded by full cheeks because she always smiled.
Her lips were painted berry and when they parted with
her soft words, you felt loved. Her legs were covered in
silken panty hose or else bare. Her strength was evident
in her calves and the expanse of her hips. A cinched
waist held a skirt at her knee or just slightly above. A
blouse of a vibrant color only added to her smile. The
beauty that was my mother, always matched both inside
and outside.

Of all the things that stand out in my head about
Mom, it's her walk. Mommy had the famous walk.
You could spot it a mile away. Her short strides were
quick and she used the swing of her right arm in
particular to move the elements from impeding her
walk. This all culminated in her personal theme music,

the click clack of her stilettos either announcing her entry or signaling her exit from a room. These steps were like a heartbeat. They told me that when Mommy was off doing "womanly things" with Daddy and when she was coming home from work to do the family thing. This soundtrack played so often in my head that I now imitate this in the way I walk. When my childlike foot finally reached the size of 7.5, I was able to reconnect with my mother and to match her pace to my heart beat through her shoes. This is the sound "click clack" that everyone hates. That is my lullaby, the sound of my mother's footsteps. It is a song I will never hear again.

As tight as I was to tell about the death of my mother, it also felt like a heavy weight lifted off my shoulders. There is awesome power in truth!

Guilty

    I never really cared for Nia. She always seemed like she could not be bothered with high school and especially not freshmen. Nia managed to surprise me with the revelation about her stilettos.

    I felt bad for Nia and the loss of her mom. Most of all I felt guilty for hating on the girl and them damn shoes. I felt so pathetic. I guess I really hated Nia because she appeared so much like a woman. She reminds me of my own mother. Without even realizing, I was projecting the frustration I feel towards my own mother onto Nia.

    Honestly, I never understood what the big deal was during that first week of school when I joined the crowd of other students and eagerly awaited the sound of the click clack. Even though more than half the school was annoyed by the sound of Nia's footsteps, no one dared to confront her. Tre was the only person with enough heart to approach the issue even indirectly. Funny thing, Tre never even heard the response to the bag of worms she opened. Even more strange is that

Aw Shucks !

Nia might feel thankful for revealing the burden of her heart and the mystery of her stilettos.

Nia's unveiling gave me some perspective. No matter how little she is around, at least I have a mother. If Nia could be strong enough to live without a mother, I could actually be strong enough to engage my own. I plan to actually be awake when my mother looks in on me tonight. I am going to ask her to go shopping with me. I guess this is what mothers and daughter do.

Girl Talk

I was not kidding when I said I was going to engage my mother. I wrote my mom a sticky note and left it on the hall table where she leaves her keys. I crumbled almost ten sheets trying to pen the perfect note. I did not want to appear sugary or desperate, just friendly. Dang, I didn't even know how to begin an exchange with my own mother! Just when I thought I would ditch the mother and daughter idea, I thought of Nia. She was my motivation. I realize I may not always have the time to be uncomfortable. Eventually, like Nia's mother, we all depart this Earth. I decided to write the following note in the end:

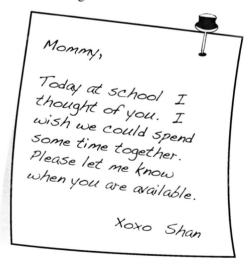

Diary of a Little Diva

Aw Shucks !

I prayed when I left the note for my Mom. I felt brave and triumphant. I was proud of myself for being honest. I knew she would appreciate me addressing her as Mommy. This was much warmer than my usual reference- mother. If I was ever going to get close to my mom, I had to start somewhere.

I could barely sleep. I was like a child waiting on the tooth fairy. I imagined my mom would at first be baffled. Then she would read the note. She would place the love note near her heart before she walked into the room for us to engage in girl talk.

"Shannon," mother whispered.

"Yes"

"Can we chat?" She asked tentatively.

"Of course," I responded like I was talking to a friend. I even made a space on the bed for her to sit and encourage our conversation.

Seated mother asked, "What happened at school today? Are you okay?"

"Yes, I am okay. I found out my classmates mother passed. It made me think of you"

"Oh," she gasped. "Shannon, I am so sorry."

It had been such a long time since she had held me next to her. I was drowning in her perfume. I did not remember her touch. Her embrace was both beautiful and foreign.

"Baby, I was so delighted to receive your note" mother continued. She looked around my room trying to take it all in. It was not often that mom was in my space with maximum light.

"So what do you propose we do for fun?

"I was thinking bra shopping, I could use a little help. I don't think Dad can handle that trip"

She showed her radiant smile when she responded, "You're right about that. How about tomorrow?"

"Perfect," I squealed.

Comforted by this conversation, I slept well with sweet dreams of mother and I and our girl talk.

Diary of a Little Diva

Victoria's Secret

I knew it. The reason why I hate people especially females, is because they always disappoint you. The two females closest to me, Lea and my mom, had already proven this. After mother had agreed to go shopping and even suggested the day she cancelled. The note had the nerve to be brief.

Pumpkin,

I had a work emergency. It's the case I have been working on with the young girl. See the attached article for more info.

Mom

This heifer had the nerve to call me Pumpkin AND give me homework. I swear, I can't stand her. She didn't even think that I asked her to go shopping for a reason. Maybe I had a real problem. I don't know how to buy bras. She should be helping me. Screw her job. I am a young girl, how about working on your daughter's case. "Pumpkin, I had an emergency." I can't believe her. And calling me Pumpkin. That made me furious.

Tweet: Cruella Deville has been replaced by a new villaneous woman- Zena Brown.

In our family when a child is born they get a nickname based on the size and shape of their head. You already know that Paul is Ping Pong. When I was born, I had a big round head just like a pumpkin. Mother calling me Pumpkin took me back to a time when I did remember a connection between us.

Mother canceling our date made me feel like I was robbed at knife point. As I am walking down the street of life I pass by someone who I assume means me no harm. Then out of nowhere they just senselessly stab me. I was left bloodied and feeling vacant. I never

knew my mother would be my assailant. My tears of
pain are like blood leaving my body. I didn't know if I
was more shocked or angry. I crumbled the sticky note
into the tiniest ball imaginable and threw it in the kitchen
garbage that was discarded daily.

Determined to celebrate my physical growth, I
decided to venture bra shopping alone. I had not really
expected my mother to be by my side anyway. Mother's
presence was a special and rare occasion. It just would
have been nice to share this experience with my mom.
I waited as long as I could for this moment. I was well
on my way to success in high school; I had successfully
escaped from the Alcatraz of Pops and big brother, I
checked out the lay of the land in my new school, had
established a connect with cool people and according to
my cousin, "The Perv", my summer t-shirts and the boob
development project were well underway. So I did it,
finally. Oh I hope you're not thinking the big "it." The
"it" I'm talking about now is bra shopping at Victoria's
Secret.

Bra shopping was so exciting. I tried on almost
all the designs and colors. I wanted to rip my shirt open

like Superman and proudly display my newly developed chest. However, I thought it best to just get some new bras.

I was no baller like D$, but I had enough bread to come home with a few nice undergarments displayed in the famous pink and white shopping bag. Oh to be a C-cup; a girl could only dream.

Baller (n) A high level of social and financial status where one was put on a pedestal and highly regarded. *Ex. By the make of his suit, I can tell that he is a baller.*

Bread (n) A colloquial term meaning money. Synonyms: dough, cash, mullah, stocks, paper, guap. *Ex. She spent a lot of bread at the mall.*

My Bday

When your birthday is in September and you are at a new school, you gets no love. So last year I quietly ushered in becoming 14 with the family. This included the trifling note from my ever absent mother saying "many more."

This year, I had Nikki and Corey to celebrate with and I had Nia too. I wanted to celebrate my bday in style. Honestly, people were very attracted to me, both male and female, and I just didn't know what to do with the attention. Not to toot my own horn but Beep, Beep! Do I sound conceited? Nah, it's not like that. All those damn magazines, my Aunt T, Ms. L and even Oprah are always talking about esteem, so just think of me as holding myself in high esteem.

Sophomore year did not begin with summer school as Freshmen year did. Of course, I still hung out with Corey & Nikki, my dynamic duo. The train was our bat cave, and the halls of SFU were our Gotham City. Though small fish in this mega pond, we held our own.

Aw Shucks !

Us passing in the halls warranted various types of greetings from the cheerleader like yelps of freshmen, who know a sister had book smarts and street credibility. We especially loved the mad proper and sincere greetings we got from other sophomores. It was like an NBA All-Star game with people shouting your name, both your full government and your crew dubbed name.

Government(n)- The name that is issued to you and noted on your birth certificate. This is the name by which the government recognizes you for tax purposes. *Ex. Yo, why are you shouting my government across the hall?*

Folks were jockeying to get a locker next to yours, hoping for the chance of a verbal exchange or the occasional cheek air smooch from those you truly missed over the summer. Your real peoples you kept in touch with whether or not school was in session. I could easily see why juniors were damn near celebrities. As a sophomore, I felt like the greetings were the mob of the paparazzi trying to get a piece of me. It felt damn good.

We all knew we would be there. Nikki, Corey and I. There was no need for all the over excited squeezes, like we hadn't seen each other in two months of summer break. That shit wasn't gonna happen.

We had grown even closer over the summer. My father is proof of this. You know that if my conservative, business man, nobody is good enough for his baby type daddy knew my friends by their names that my crew was tight. What Pops thought was still important to me, even though I was growing up and I made good decisions. Besides I told Pops that I had learned my grasshopper lessons well. He had to trust me to experience life a little.

For real though, I was glad he approved of my circle of friends. Even now I get tickled thinking of how my high school experiences would be different without Corey and Nikki. I knew I would see them beyond the end of our four years, marked by our high school graduation. There was room for more friends and there was never jealousy, it was all love. I had two more members in my family.

The good thing about school, in addition to all the learning crap and social aspects, were the birthday celebrations. My birthday is September 9th.

Aw Shucks !

The timing couldn't be better. Everyone was over the joy and blues of the first day. Some people had already expended their wardrobes and the pettiness of trying to impress others, but September was still too early for any dances or major games. My bday became the first jump off of the year.

Jump off (n) - Something that acts as a catalyst, the motivating force for subsequent events. *Ex. Thanksgiving is usually the jump off for seasonal weight gain.*

Eventually, I would be the business. For right now I was going to enjoying becoming 15!

Aw Shucks !

Sept 9th 6 am

My earthday day! The day God saw fit for me to be on Earth began like any other. The alarm sounded, I smacked it for an additional snooze. Ten minutes later I woke to something bumping on the radio that would stay in my head all day.

6:10 am

Today I awakened with enthusiasm. Usually I am a lazy bum, hitting the snooze button at least two, sometimes even three times. Thank goodness I lay out three outfits every night. Y'all know my Dad taught me that with his tight ass. Before I get into anything else, I bend my knees in prayer. I always give thanks for my life and ask for a positive, safe and productive day. Today I especially asked for balance cuz the outfits I picked all required that I wear a heel. For me this was like a hooker stiletto. This might be a challenge. Despite watching Nia, I couldn't mess with any stilettos yet. Amen.

Aw Shucks !

6:20 am

The music from the alarm clock is blaring again and my head is bobbing to the beat. I run my fingers over my scarf to find my Doobie Pins still in place. This means my tedious evening routine of brushing and pinning my hair so it to falls perfectly, is working. I give thanks again. Can't have bedhead on my earthday. I don't usually care what people think, but with the pumps I intended to wear, that might make people look at me strangely. My clothing was usually stylish, but for the new year in my life, I wanted to try a new type of shoe. I wanted the onlookers to notice my new style and to comment positively, not to laugh.

I was glad to reach the shower before my brother so I could languish under the water. I am fully alive because of the sound of water. The steady stream of warmth and the aroma of my vanilla soap are like my coffee. I sponge dry to avoid dehydrating my skin, then I apply a light coat of baby oil all over my body. To my face I add moisturizer. With my hair pins removed and a squirt of smell well, I am ready for the day.

Aw Shucks !

6:40 am

"Shug, Shug, Come down stairs." The booming voice of my Dad commanded that I show my face immediately. The bark of his voice was like that of a Chihuahua. These are little dogs that make a lot of noise because it's their nature, but they are real sweethearts. I hurried nonetheless. "I'm coming Pops," I shouted. Shug is what most of the family calls me, short for sugar.

The story goes that I was no bigger than a 5 pound bag of sugar and dad carried me the same way he used to carry around a bag of sugar between his wrist and forearm. Mother said he carried it and me delicately because of his own fondness for goodies. He didn't believe in wasting sugar. I guess the sweetness still carries because I love me some Pops. After Pops started calling me Shug, it just stuck. His calling me Shug or even Kam Shan (his other nickname for me) was cool. I only worried when he called me by my full government. Not to keep my favorite guy waiting, I called again, "Give me five minutes." I needed to make an appearance. After all, it was my earthday. "Hurry up!" Pops called back.

Aw Shucks !

6:48 am

Today the color green won out of the outfit choices. I chose green for prosperity and wealth. I rocked it with chocolate, who doesn't love chocolate? (Don't answer that question.) My top was a printed pattern with mostly green along with dark chocolate jeans and matching heels. For my ears, I wore green chandelier earrings and a coordinating bracelet for my right wrist. On the left I wore nothing. No time piece, I hated time restrictions. Oops, can't forget to get my lip gloss poppin' in chocolate shine.

I was a 15 year old Hershey Kiss in the perfect wrapper. I gave thanks once more and almost killed myself on the six steps that separated upstairs from downstairs.

7:05 am

"Morning Daddy," I shouted and waited with my girlish smile for his reaction to my outfit. My smile was wide-eyed and approval seeking. His beaming reaction was all I needed to feel confident. "Look at my Shug. You are growing up." When he reached in to

Diary of a Little Diva

embrace me, I had to warn him not to wrinkle my outfit.

"Daddy, watch my gear," I cried. He retorted, "Whatever, Shug." I couldn't believe it, Pops was trying to be cool. I just laughed until I made the snort sound. How embarrassing. "Daddy, See what you made me do." Maybe he wasn't so tight afterall.

Pops stood in the foyer. He looked at me for another five minutes, while I gathered my bag, jacket and weeble wobbled to the door. He couldn't contain his laughter. As usual Daddy rescued me saying, "Since it's your birthday and it seems like you are struggling, how about I chauffeur you today." My head was screaming, Hell yeah. My mouth responded, "Thanks."

Just walking downstairs and to the door in those heels already had me exhausted. The last thing I needed on my earthday was to look like a fake ass supermodel. Not today. So just in case the heels didn't work out and to avoid any potential embarrassment, you know I had equally cute pair of flat shoes to go with my outfit. During the car ride I prayed for balance, literally. My walk was so sad I even let Pops drop me at the school door.

The day was almost perfect until my descent from

the car when Pops passed me a sticky note. I knew it was from my mother. The note said, "Happy birthday baby." Ewww, I swear I can't stand her. I was so tight, but not even she could ruin today. I crumbled the note in my hand and kissed Pops, "I love you, man."

7:25 am

Getting my head straight, I remembered, Aw shucks, I was 15 today! In my head I began what I hope was a confident stride to the tune of "Today is your birthday." My personal concert was interrupted by snickering. At first I ignored it knowing it was not for me until I heard the laughter again and closer to me. It was coming from Ms. Thang as she was called for wearing stilettos to the tune of click clack. Today was no different except that she was laughing at me.

With an extension of her hand for assistance Nia told me to meet her at Ms. L's room as soon as I got into the building. With a 'see you later Shan' she was off with the famous click clack fading in the background, but more importantly, she was offering much needed help.

My heels were certainly not making a click

clack melody. I sounded more like a stampede of elephants as I hiked to Ms. L's room. I followed through on the invitation to meet up because I knew it was nothing like a gang initiation, drugs or her making a move on me. When I finally reached, Nia was laughing again and honestly, I knew why.

"Do I look that bad?"

"Yeah, Girl, You look like a hot mess, but I got you."

This could be the start of something especially since she didn't use that lame ass line "I got your back." I just hated that line.

Nia, resumed the lesson of the day by saying, "Please tell me you have a pair of sensible flats with you."

"Of course" I responded.

"Next, don't carry any extra books today" Nia advised. She noted that this would further throw me off balance. She removed my coordinating bracelet to my other wrist explaining that I didn't want to risk getting anything caught on my bag.

"And for Pete's sake, if you get any balloons,

please don't carry them yourself. Ask your friends to help. Your job today is to shine and balance on them shoes not to be clouded by balloons and end up tripping."

"Okay, no extra books. Let Corey hold my balloons. Anything else?" I asked eagearly.

"Yes," Nia recalled. "Go to the bathroom every period. As soon as you are in the hall put on your flats, run to the bathroom and just let your feet rest for a few minutes. After lunch and a proper stroll around for photo opportunities you can retire the heels for the day."

"I can do that."

"Now we have 15 minutes left before the bell rings. You better not screw it up! "

"Damn, you sound like Ms. L."

"I have never given anyone these tips and the universe knows you needed some help, so here it goes. Watch me."

My eyes were crazy glued to her movement. It was like she was gliding not stomping at a sorority step show. Her arms gently swung back and forth giving her balance and the appearance of grace. Most of all Nia

Diary of a Little Diva

warned, "Take your time. Today you are how old?"

I couldn't hide my excitement when I squealed "15."

"Today, you want to be seen as a woman of the future. Walk slow and confident, pause as you need to receive wishes, and balance off whichever leg is stronger to give the other foot a rest. Use your arms to direct you and for balance. Don't run and don't drag your feet, Nia admonished."

"Okay, Okay," I said taking it all in. I got this. I prayed for balance today, I just didn't know that it was going to come from Ms. Nia.

"Let me see what you got." I did the mental check list with bracelets switched and dropped my science book as I began my strut.

"Not too bad," was the report from Nia. She finally warned me not to switch my ass because everything would move naturally when you are in balance. I tried it again and even added a turn.

"How about now?" I asked.
After ten takes, I got the nod of approval coupled with a

"Not bad kid. What period is your lunch?"

I answered, "fifth."

"See me in the second floor bathroom so I can show you how to enter for lunch."

"Okay." We separated to attend class.

"Hey Nia", I called from behind, "Thanks."

"No problem. Work it birthday girl."

I made a mental note that Nia walked with balance using her arms to guide her. The arms were close to the body, they did not swing wide or swift. Like me, Nia's feet were not perfectly straight when she walked her right foot pointed out slightly, but she still worked it. Her head was high and the sound echoed click clack, click clack, click clack. I would copy this behavior.

V-card

In high school and sometimes even before, there is pressure to be cool and do certain things. I remember one time, in 7th grade, these girls said I couldn't hang out with them unless I had a V-card. I had no idea what a V-card was, but I found out pretty quickly. The next day I came with what looked like a driver's license that had my picture and the word V-card across the top. On the back it had the definition of a *V* for virgin, yes a virgin! When I asked them to see their V-cards, they had nothing to show. Let's just say we never really became friends.

In high school you didn't engage in show and tell, you kind of went off your instinct, who gave you a good or bad vibe. So far I was vibing with Dominique, Corey and Nia.

Dominique... she was a story I still couldn't fully tell because I was still trying to figure it out. What I did know was that Nikki could hold her own. She wasn't quite a dime, but she definitely had dime potential. Her attire was always proper. Nikki was especially fond of labels, but also mixed and matched well. Hey, if you had

good taste you could mix Juicy with Walmart. If your
parents would tight on cash, you could make Target
a boutique, and call it Tarjay. This is how I flow. A
little of this and a little of that. In the end, I just want
to be myself and not look like a clone or worse a damn
clown.

Corey, That's still my boy with his cute self.
That smile just makes me melt. Of course, I could
never tell him that. If he ever knew that I, Shannon
Kameron Brown, was even remotely interested in him
romantically...his head would friggin swell up like the
new years' blimp. He might need a personal assistant
to have him carry his big ego around. I can't stand him
and that damn smile.

Also in my crew occasionally was Nia. I owe
Nia a lot. She really helped a sister get her stroll on
in her heels on my birthday. If how I walked from the
car into the school was any indication of how my day
was going to go, I would have easily fallen on my ass
or worse my lovely face. To that you can't help but
say, Aw Shucks! Imagine this loveliness splattered like
pieces of a puzzle. Let's not go there! Getting back to

Aw Shucks !

Nia... She is the only chick in high school that wears stilettos like a grown woman. She rescued my sorry behind and helped me put on quite a birthday show.

Today for some reason I had an odd feeling. I don't know if it was excitement or anxiety. I just knew something big was going to happen. I always listen to that feeling inside of me. Right before lunch we always meet in the bathroom to reapply lip gloss. Dominique and I catch up before we have to deal with the mob in the lunchroom. While in the bathroom that feeling came over me again. This time the feeling was distinctly in my stomach, but I didn't think that I was due for my cycle. I checked my phone calendar and confirmed that I was still a week away from being on. When I asked Nikki if she had any Tylenol to offset my impending cramps, she said, "Hold on." While I waited, I riffled through my bag to look for my own stash because the School Nurses office acts like you are going to die if they give you one pill. What they don't realize is that they risk death if my cramps get too bad. To avoid all this drama, I take care of myself and that's why I keep a stash. I must have given my stash to someone else in need and now here I stood in need.

Aw Shucks !

Dominique finally managed to find one raggedy pill that looked suspect at best, but I needed to quell whatever I had been feeling the entire day. This feeling had escalated from my head to my stomach. I told Nikki that these cramps were kicking my butt. I don't know if it was pain or delirium but I think Dominique mumbled some crap like, "At least you got cramps." Now along with my stomach flip flopping, my head was spinning and my mouth almost said, Aw shucks!

Before either Dominique or I said another word, I dropped to the floor to make sure there were no feet or ears overhearing our conversation. For extra measure and any case of eavesdropping, I pushed in each stall door to make sure nobody was trying to get in on my girls' business. After this, I grabbed Dominique's hand and went into the last stall also known as the Girl's Sanctuary. In this case, the conference room. Nikki put the toilet lid down to provide a comfortable seat and immediately covered her face with her hands. She knew damn well that I heard what she had mumbled about cramps. With Dominique seated, I took the counselors position and paced the floor while watching the door before the lunchtime bumrush.

With only a few minutes to spare for discussion, I just plainly asked,

"Dom Why would you not have cramps? We always flow together, so If I'm about to be on so should you, right?"

"I guess," was Nikki's weak reply.

Astonished I responded, "What do you mean you guess?

Did your cycle start early? Are you so stressed that it is affecting your flow? Things are cool at home, right?"

"Yeah the family is good, but my flow ain't."

I searched my mental Rolodex to try to understand what Dominique was telling me, but I could not wrap my head around the conclusion I had reached. I know that I was a proud V-card carrier! Then I thought everyone may not have a Virgin Card including Dominique. I pleaded with Dominique to just tell me what was up with about as much cool as I could muster. I certainly didn't want to panic Nikki with my inexperience or make her feel judged.

With her head still bowed on the toilet seat, she

just popped up and said "Let's meet at our office before we go to lunch."

With this new meeting location and a whirling head, I rushed back to class, got my books, and sent a text for Corey to collect us some grub. I told him we had girl issues and would be late. Corey knew us so well he even knew when we had our cycle. He got so tired of us complaining about pain and acting evil that he even resorted to carrying a stash of pills. He said, "You know I only do this for my ladies. I don't even go to the store to get my mom her lady products. Y'all got me tripping."

Damn, he is just so cute and smart. I think I love him. I mean, that's our boy. This Nikki thing really has me tripping.

Trippin - Relates to the drug or situational induced state that alters normal mental thought processes or shock. *Ex. The news about their divorce had everyone trippin.*

I was off to staircase B, between the second and third floor, just above the principal's office. This was the location of our office. Our rationalization for choosing this location was because of the discretion it provided. Why not above the principal's office? We were ladies conducting serious business. Other people were too loud or dumb to hold an office in this spot. The school cameras had limited access and for three people you could squeeze into the corners and have an intimate conversation. This was perfect for our crew. I have to give Corey credit for spying out this spot. He got the scoop because of that beautiful smile.

Corey did get played once. Corey tells the story that it was about a month into the second semester and he was running late to class when a chocolate bar of a sweet girl called out to him. He said he thought she was Mrs. Goodbar herself and could not resist.

She said, "What's up?"

Corey answered confidently, "I'm good, What's up with you ma?"

She replied, "I need your help."

And being the gentleman he is Corey asked, "How may I help you?"

Corey followed her lead as she dragged him by

the hand to the space between the second and third floor in staircase B. Then she planted the sweetest kiss on top of that adorable smile leaving my boy dazed. This is how our office space was discovered.

After tasting his smile, Mrs. Goodbar seemed to have disappeared. We don't speak of this matter.

Now safely in our office space, I demanded that Dominique tell me what the hell was going on. She was not forthcoming with the information, so I had to pry.

I first began by repeating my questions of earlier concerning stress and the family, "Are you okay? Things good at home?"

Dominique responded in the most annoyed voice, almost screaming, "Are you serious?"

"Well, let's stop playing these guessing games and just tell me what the hell is going on."

In an effort to lighten the mood, I jokingly added, "If you don't have your cycle then you must be pregnant, You slut bag."

Just as I began to giggle knowing that my girl was no slut, she said, "Yeah I might be."

The room froze. We just stood there like

mannequins unable to move. The only movement was the overpowering thump of my heart. Now I was really pacing. Okay, she has no cramps, obviously she is not a virgin and now she might be pregnant, WTF!

"Okay, Nikki, I need a minute here. Are you saying that you might be pregnant? From who? When? Where did you find the time to lose your virginity? Shit, This is for real girl."

"Yes Princess, while you spent most of the year worrying about friends, I have been doing other things. And no, I wasn't a virgin. Mack is not the first guy I have been with."

"Who in the freak is Mack? Have you mentioned him before? If we usually chill, When do you hang with him? And don't call me Princess, Slut bag."

This time we laughed together but not for humor in the comments, we laughed mostly to keep from crying. I might be a V-card carrying member, but even a virgin knows a little bit about preparations if you are ready to get busy. Of course, there were condoms both male and female, spermicides, a host of pills, the patch, the new IUD and the morning after pill. We were going to explore the last option for Nikki if we were in the right time frame. If necessary, I would even call my mother for some advice. She does at least answer my phone calls.

Beyond this knowledge, Pops made the rest quite simple.

He said, "Your body is growing and I know you are feeling different emotions. You might even get horny. When you decide to give yourself to someone don't let it be because he says I love you. No one loves you more that me, your brother and your uncles. Don't let a clown say that you are beautiful and have your clothes fall off. You will always be my princess, and especially don't let some joker say that you all will be together forever. When you decide, let it be for your own reasons and use protection. If you want to know anything more about sex, talk to your mother."

This advice has stayed with me and just like Pops suspected, these young boys tried to pull all those lines on me. Truthfully, I have only really had one kiss. I even think of kissing Corey. I can't yet imagine doing anything else.

Aw Shucks !

Selfishly, I assured Dominique that all would be well and that we would solve her problem after the pep rally. At least being focused on having fun would keep her mind off the possibility of pregnancy. Pops would understand all the excitement and imagine that I would be home later than usual. This would give me a chance to go to the clinic with Nikki.

Sticky Notes

I didn't even know how to begin a conversation with my own mother, especially one of a sexual nature, so I just blurted it out. To add insult to injury I wrote on her famous mode of communication, sticky notes. My note said:

Hey, I have a ? concerning a friend, what should one do if their period is late? I think it has only been a day or two since the "act."

While writing the note, I was sad for my girl, but delirious about the pep rally. Is that bad?

I also felt a sense of annoyance that I had to be so unsure communicating with my own Mom. I wished she and I had the type of relationship I had with Pops. I just wasn't comfortable talking to Dad about sex, much less pregnancy. If Daddy had even heard the word pregnancy, he would probably faint. I felt safe because I knew the note wasn't about me.

The note seemed distant, like I was writing to a stranger. This was the reality of the relationship between my mother and I, distant.

You could imagine my surprise when at 12:08 am the light in the hallway let in more light than usual. I could tell she was reading the sticky note I had left in the hallway near where my mother always puts her keys. Almost immediately thereafter, the door to my bedroom opened and let in more light.

She called out to me, "Shannon, baby it's Mommy. Do you want to talk?" She paused a beat before she continued, "I know like most nights that you pretend to be asleep. I wrote you a note and you should be prepared to talk in the morning. Good night."

"Night," I called as my mother neared the hallway again.

I didn't expect to be emotional, but I was. I was

Diary of a Little Diva

excited to know that my Mom was so responsive to my note. She was receptive and available. Maybe if I went to her more she would also respond positively. My only question was, Why was I going to her, rather than her coming to me? Now I wondered even more what the note said.

When Mom had safely passed, I collected the note from the hall and read it. It said

> Shan,
>   I trust that ur ok and that situation is truly about a friend. Here is a number to a place that can help #917.555.5555 or google for more info.

On a second sticky note she wrote:

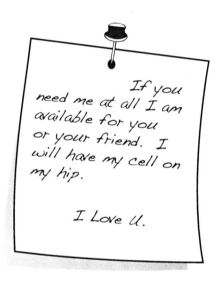

If you need me at all I am available for you or your friend. I will have my cell on my hip.

I Love U.

    I can't front, reading those sticky notes made me feel good. To know that my mother really did love me. I stayed up after reading the notes to do my research. I found a clinic that said counselors were available to help you learn about your cycle and birth control options. It was there to make women feel empowered about their bodies. Okay, this sounded progressive and also like the Sex 101 refresher Nikki needed. I made an appointment using a fake name. A combination of my and Nikki's names. So Nikki Brown had a 4pm appointment at Ladies First.

Aw Shucks !

I sent a text message to tell Nikki that I had gotten some information and that we had an appointment the next day at 4pm. I knew she would appreciate it. I also promised that I would keep her entertained for the Pep Rally. From the beginning of the day until about 3pm, the fun was on, and thereafter it was business.

I could not wait until tomorrow! I knew it was going to be an Aw Shucks kind of day. First the Nikki thang, then the notes from Mom, not to mention Nia's surprise. I planned to wake up early and go to Nikki's house to get dressed. We were each other's support, especially given her emotional state.

I was also trying to avoid an early chat with my mother at all costs. What if I didn't say the right thing. What if she hated my style of dress? I could do a quick midnight chat or a sticky note, but she wanted to talk to me. What would I say to her? Should I tell her I hate her job and that we all feel neglected. That she should be lucky Pops doesn't leave her butt. Should I tell my mother that beyond a sticky note, I don't know what to say to her.

As I scribbled a message on a sticky note telling my mom I would call if I needed her she called my name. "Shannon, Shannon," but I was ghost. I shouted back, "Later Ma."

 Ghost (v) - to quickly disappear
Ex. When we heard sirens, we were ghost.

Pep Rally

It was going to be one heck of a day. I was
amped the see all the team in full uniform. I was ready
to laugh at staff trying to reclaim their youth. I was
most excited to just be a part of the scene. The long
awaited pep rally was here and then it was only one
more day for a long holiday. The holiday meant that
clock in my bedroom would not alarm with blaring
music to wake me from the sleep I had not enough of. I
would especially need some sleep after all the thinking
I had been doing about the Pep Rally. Thoughts about
how I would behave, who I would see and even what I
would wear.

My outfit got the most consideration of my time
since I was going to debut a new look. I had quite a
reputation of being a female who thought she was all
that or the business as some were known to say. You
could imagine the other names I had been called, but
none to my face. I could only imagine what people
thought with their blank stares, rolling eyes and tightly

pressed lips that never emitted utterances in the form of any greeting. I am Nia and that has absolute meaning. If I were listed in the dictionary with a picture, you would find sweet brown girl that rarely smiles and always wears stilettos; well one pair of stilettos in particular. These shoes are much like my security blanket. But so few people know this because school dynamics dictated that one cannot be vulnerable or else someone would sense it, expose it, and attempt to devour you. I was hell bent on not becoming anyone's lunch so I kept my secrets in my breast, close to my own heart. Sometimes I cry myself to sleep wishing my mother was here. Her voice alone, her scent, or the famous click clack of her stilettos I now wear, would soothe me and put me in a place of peace.

Back to the Pep Rally. Let me paint the picture of what a Pep Rally looks like... the auditorium bleachers are filled like Yankee Stadium. It's the bottom of the 9th inning. The crowd is on their feet and the top batter is at the mound. He already has two strikes against him. We all pray that in the next pitch he will hit a homerun. We wait with baited breath...this is the excitement of a Pep Rally.

Aw Shucks !

The athletes are plotting on which girl to score
with and girls are coveting the Jerseys and jewelry of
jocks. This day, all eyes are wide open watching for
break-ups, new couples and the latest fashion trends.
This is probably one of only a few days where there
is 100% attendance. You are most unfortunate if you
don't have a camera or a crew to roll with because what
your eyes will witness are definite conversation starters.
I can't make this stuff up.

When there is a Pep Rally the halls are brightly
decorated with posters, shout outs and announcements
from teams and club meetings. Teachers even get in on
the action by posting student challenges to engage in
debate. Ms. McKay had posted some quote by Oprah
that said "Breathe. Let go. And remind yourself that this
very moment is the only one you know you have for
sure." I was digging it and wanted to debate the idea,
but who the hell was I going to mention that to? You bet
your ass – no one! This is the same crazy Ms. L that
dared that if all of her students passed the midterm with
an 85% that she would get on the desk and dance to a
song of the student's choice. You know I helped some

students study for that exam right? To see Ms. L, the quintessential lady on the desk dancing...OMG!

Mr. Brown the counselor who thinks he can ball, was trying to rally some support for a teacher vs. student basketball game. There were definitely some takers. We were all just scared to think of what the teachers looked like in shorts much less running up and down the court. For safety purposes I hope that the fashion police and EMS are on hand. This situation could get ugly quick.

The Pep Rally, like the lunchroom, was segregation by self-selection at its best. Beyond the typical athlete/cheerleader, you also had much like Spike Lee's "Do the Right Thing" The Wannabe's, The Outsiders, The Beautiful Ones, GDI's, that is Goddamn Individuals, and the Random Folks. I could have fit into any category. I guess I was mostly a GDI, but with the constant stares and the mention of my name you might have thought otherwise. Today I was doing something totally new. Well, several new things: not wearing stilettos and chilling with Shannon and her crew.

You remember Shan, the poor thing trying to balance some pumps on her birthday. I had to teach homegirl how to walk with confidence and to pose without posing and without killing herself. This was no easy feat! Now it was her turn to help me out. We decided that I would look like a typical high school student. Now everyone knows average is so beneath me, but I wanted the stares that were beaming into my soul to not make me feel like an outcast. I wanted to feel connected with other young people. Perhaps I could tolerate them if they weren't too damn silly or immature. After much magazine, catalog, and on-line shopping consultation, I purchased my first pair of sneakers and skinny jeans. With Shan's help, I looked youthful but still had flare, something that still said Nia. Of course, I wore colors to compliment the mocha of my complexion and we should all know you are never fully dressed without a smile. With my shoulders back, head up, Nike Shox laced, and jeans hugging, I strutted into the building. There was no theme music of my stilettos. No click clack, click clack but I was still Nia to a new beat.

Nikki, Shannon's homegirl, was a bit odd. For all the talk Shannon did about her crew, Corey seemed scared or maybe that was a crush I saw and Nikki was just out of it. I was up for a complete make-over including the company I sought, so nothing was going to ruin my day. The Pep Rally was a chance for me to show my true self.

My debut was a hit! Everyone responded so positively. People smiled and I even initiated a few "Hellos." I wonder if they even knew that I was the same person.

There was only one point during the day that I had wished for my signature click clack. Around mid-day, I had forgotten the usual bathroom lip gloss refresher that Shannon and Nikki do, so I made it to our destination a little late. Most people might find it difficult to walk in stilettos, but I was having trouble moving in flats. When I finally reached the bathroom, there seemed to be a crowd. Not to draw any attention to myself, I fell back and kept a watchful eye. In the midst of the crowd I recognized Shannon. If my eyes were not playing tricks on me I would have sworn some girls were pressing her and treating Shannon like freshmeat. I held back a bit longer, not wanting to punk Shannon and to be clear about what was going on.

Shannon seemed either unaware or unconcerned about what was going on around her. She continued to look in the mirror and focused on her lip gloss. When her pout was to her satisfaction she issued a firm, "Excuse me" to exit the bathroom. When one girl was reluctant to move, Shannon said, "I believe I said excuse me." The girl was no longer hesitant and stepped aside. I entered in the path that Shannon had exited and resumed her spot in the mirror. As our paths crossed I gave the same cue Ms. L had given me a while back and winked. With the return wink, I knew everything was cool and said, "I'll meet you outside in a minute." I was not about to let these birds throw us any further off schedule. When I left the bathroom there was no click clack to confirm that I was me, Nia. It was almost as if in silence I had created a new self.

Leaving the bathroom I felt a little confused about my own steps. I reconnected with Shannon and asked, "What was up with you and those birds?" "Nothing, I guess they were just hating my style."

"RU ready for Round 2?" Shannon asked.

I confirmed "Ready." We both said, "Aw

Diary of a Little Diva

Shucks" and laughed our way down the hall.

Bird(n)- A group of females that hang together. The females are characterized as loud and unsophisticated. *Ex. Please do not say anything like that again, you sound like a bird.*

Lady Gaga had nothing on me, the stares and glares of the paparazzi had me pumped. I didn't come off of this high until after three when Nikki reminded me of our four o'clock appointment. She had kept her end of the deal by trying to have fun at the Pep Rally and now I had to do my part as a friend.

"Nikki, Meet me at my locker. Let me say bye to Nia and our boy."

I told Corey that Nikki and I had to hurry home to finish a project. He just looked at me like I was crazy. I knew I was caught in my lie. I would IM him later to explain. I also lied to Nia when I told her I would chat later because I had cramps.

When I started walking toward our usual bus stop route, Nikki said, "Nah, Come this way. I drove today."

"What do you mean, you drove today?"

"I hope you know how to drive because I am nervous as hell."

"I have taken some lessons," was all I could muster in response.

Once I got behind the wheel and adjusted everything it all came back to me. With Nikki barking directions at me, we reached the clinic in 15 minutes before our scheduled appointment.

Once inside the waiting area, during the one hour wait, I noticed the area was bright. It was filled with female celebrities. They had been part of the got milk campaign and other positive images of women. We had to fill out the requisite paper work and wait to be called. I filled out the info too, using a fake name of course so Nikki would not feel awkward. With our paperwork complete, we were guided down the hall and lectured. We were requested to pee on a stick and for extra measure, we were issued the morning after pill. I watched as Nikki almost choked trying to ingest the pill without water. I secured my dose in my purse to add to my stash. With a sigh of relief we rushed toward the door.

Nikki was called back from our speedy exit by the receptionist. The nurse's aide explained that Nikki's pregnancy test was a false negative and that she would have to return in a week to see if her hormone levels had changed. This definitely encouraged me to hold onto my V-card just a little longer. Nikki asked if I would come with her next week just to check and I agreed. We walked out feeling the heaviness of motherhood instead of the cheer of the Pep Rally.

Transfer

The pep rally had already set the stage for some major players and identified new minor players at SFU. As expected, some relations were blossoming and others dissolving. I was in the blossoming category. I had not realized that Nia's debut without her stilettos would impact me, but it did. This along with how I refused to let females get at me in the bathroom made people think I had heart I was told. Truth is, I don't pay females any attention, so at first I did not even realize that the girls in the bathroom were pressuring me. Turns out, the Pep Rally was more than just a voyeuristic experience. Nia became less dependent on her shoes; Nikki was not going to be a mother, I hoped and I was becoming more comfortable with myself.

We were ready for the world.

We cruised the hallways as usual, greeting acquaintances and acknowledging others. We kept our lip gloss meeting and had identified Ms. L's wink as the distress signal. We were basking in all our glory, that is, until after 11am. We were surprised by a new face. We did a double check to try to identify the face. Was it a parent? The attire was not that of a guest speaker. When we saw the face again during the change of classes we had to deduce that the new face was a transfer student.

Heads whipped around in a double take. One looked a second time, because they wanted to be sure that they had seen something special. It was as if a celebrity was passing but you recognized their star quality despite the sunglasses. The movement in the halls was very similar to the way it was when I was first introduced to Ms. Nia via her stiletto click clack. Since Nia was standing there with me, I really wondered what was going on. I sharpened my gaze on the new face and those surrounding me. More interesting than the sighting of this new face was Ms. Thang's reaction. The click clack of Nia's stiletto stopped, not paused and she sighed. The sigh was followed by an emphatic and surprised "Damn!"

Y'all know I said, "Aw Shucks!"

It was like a scene out of Maury Povich on paternity test Tuesday where the guests had you looking from side-to-side wondering when something was going to pop off. My mouth was open because I could not believe that Ms. Cool as a Cucumber dka Nia would even remotely be interested in a high school student. I guess what Mama says about learning something new everyday finally applied to my life because this was definitely some new stuff. Now it was cutie pies move. What was he going to do? I wondered. My head was swinging from left to right in anticipation of how this was going to play out.

Before too many more spectators could comment on the scene, Nia caught her hand to her mouth surprised by her own reaction. What she didn't realize was that her thoughts of delight in this man had already translated into sound and action. She was wondering how she could shift the attention away from herself. She was used to the attention of long critical gazes, but these stares were different. These were not the usual I can't stand her because she is so cute. This was the, Aw Shucks what will happen next stare. No turning back now she had done the damn thing by letting her emotions show. Let the chips falls where they may.

Aw Shucks !

In an effort to encourage the chips to fall in the direction she wanted them to go, Nia walked up to the handsome specimen and said, "Hi, I'm Nia. Welcome to SFU. If you need any assistance getting around, listen out for me."

"Listen?" he asked.

"Yes, Hear me walk away." With a smile over her shoulder, the click clack rhythm filled the corridors.

Locker Drama

The slam of a locker was like the echo of a siren responding to a fire, the urgent cry of 9-1-1 or a doctor being called stat. If you don't' know the sound you might just think a person was hurriedly collecting something from their locker. If this was your guess you would be wrong, very wrong. The resonance and pitch of how a locker sounded when it was closed could be an indication of any number of things including: a budding relationship, a break-up, a failing test score, the brewing of a beat down or simple lateness to class. Which slam was this?

The slam I just heard wasn't really clear. I could usually make out what would follow strictly based on the sound. The pit of my stomach decided that something was going to happen or pop off as Corey would say. This feeling was not the usual pop quiz nervous feeling or even the sign of oncoming cramps. This feeling was heightened with a heavy sticky aroma that filled the air. The tension was weighty like grandma's homemade lemon pound cake. The only way to break this tension was to slice through it. My head just could not decide. It was between a gossip moment and somebody about to fight.

One thing about me is that I am not a rowdy chick. I watch the news. I don't want to be the news. When something breaks out, I was way far in the background. Run towards a fight? Never. Wanting to hear all the juicy bits later? For sure. Come on this is high school!

I did the whole mental navigation of what the locker slam could be, Guys? Girls? Jocks? A romantic dispute? I could not focus on my math work now, but my head was figuring the probabilities. It is Wednesday before we go on break, the lunchroom had been thick and then the slam. Not to mention that I saw what's her name with no earrings on? $X + Y =$ Aw Shucks!

The sound of kids stampeding down the hallway let you know that the gun powder had sparked. I wondered what category this locker drama would fall into, "He said, She said", "I love my Boo", "A girl fight" or just something random. Of all these dumb choices, the random acts always confused me most.

Aw Shucks !

He said, She said was the classic reason for somebody getting a beat down. Now depending on whether or not it was dudes or females, the outcome was different. When dudes fought, it was more like boxing meets a double-dutch tournament. It was the come-one, come-on, throw your hands followed by the dance move that went around it circles. When we were kids we called this a game of tag. In this scenario, some name calling might also occur along the lines of, "Oh now you're a tough guy, You gangsta now?" Most of the time the dudes looked like they needed to join a boy band or at least the dance team because they had nothing but moves.

Other times you heard fists hit face like feet to concrete. My stomach fluttered hearing the echo of a face being hit combined with slam of the locker. When guys finally did through the hands, you best believe that technology was used to record the incident. Over the airwaves using Aim messages, FaceBook postings or the lastest, Twitter the story was released to the outside world. A round 2 was always probable in these cases.

Aw Shucks !

Round 2 Translation: You did not know what was going to be waiting for you outside of any of the school doors. As innocent bystanders exited there was the potential of getting caught in the crosshairs. Innocents could become victims. At this point I prayed like hell that I was wearing neutral colors or at least colors that would not make me look like I had allegiance to any faction of people with color preferences. For once, I shouted, "Thank God" for not making me tall. I continued my prayer, "Please let my little ass escape without notice or injury." I know ass and God don't go together, but He and I have a relationship. I knew He would forgive me and understand my desperation.

There was also risk when dudes fought that others tried to get their licks in. Just like one of those TV shows when the perps knew they had a four minute window before the cops arrived. Similarly, students know the number of security guards, their posts, who is fat, who can't run, who is on the cell and who is forever at lunch. So one fight could serve to have a popcorn affect and you could go from one to five fights in under 60 seconds. Pop, pop, pop, pop off!

The least interesting kind of fight was, "I Ain't No Snitch." This is very similar to a fight between guys.

When girls thump it usually falls under a different category of He said, She said drama. It plays out like this:

Dumb girl #1: I heard from my friend, who heard from her ex, that while you was at this, that and the third place that you might have mentioned my name. All I know is that you better keep my name out your mouth!

Dumb Girl #2: (with the wave of a hand) What ever!

Dumb Girl #1: What? What did you say?

Dumb Girl #2: You heard me!

Then there is an exchange that comes from each of the girls friends in the crowd.

Crowd person #1: You gonna let her talk to you like that?

Crown person #2: I'll hold your phone and your bag girl.

Dumb Girl #1: She don't want it with me

The thing is, when one girl approaches another,

there might be some historical or underlying beef that was waiting to happen. It could also be that something happened at home and one person just needed a place to project that misplaced aggression. The tricky part is sometimes the potential fight is well watched with each girl being able to hold their own or else it ends up being a scene out of the Laundromat where someone is going to get washed.

Get washed (v): what is said about the person who loses the fight. *Ex. Yeah, Niecy had a black eye. She got washed by Cookie.*

The second and equally powerful reason, according to teenage logic of why girls fight was because, "I love my Boo."

Boo (n): A romantic or physical other in someone's life. Not to be confused with boy or girlfriend. *Ex. I was so glad that my birthday was near and that I had a Boo.*

Aw Shucks !

One's Boo status was always in a state of flux.
In high school, it could be as drastic as every class
period. Your status was especially sensitive to the
seasons. Summers are usually the time where all Boo
situations are on hiatus. It was like a major sitcom
where viewers, like students, anxiously awaited the start
of a new season.

If you are my Boo and I remotely suspect that
someone might be coming for you romantically, it was
definitely on! On meant that because of your
connection with your Boo you could be mistaken for
Lil Kim or some other chick. A chick that was down for
whatever! The old saying goes the kid gloves are off.
In this teenage drama, we say, "That's a fight on my
block." Then the ritual of removing earrings,
applying Vaseline to your face, and sending away
messages on your phone begins. This is followed by
the building of crowds in the hallway to include your
friends acting as security guards and the resident
instigator who just wanted to hype the situation.
Without question, there was always one guarantee: hair
was going to fly!

Aw Shucks !

Despite their Ali or Rocky like stances, girls rarely throw blows. The most physical contact usually involves slapping and hair pulling. You could rest assured that in a girl fight, heads would be bent, gotta stay a dime, and the arms would begin to flail in a swift and continuous motion. This my friends is the world famous windmill! The windmill has landed many a chick on the floor without weaves, scratched up and just straight washed out! The windmill had been cheated out of its rightful place in the WWE and should get honorable mention in some Hall of Fame. At the very least if deserves a shout out at a music awards show. Come on, the windmill is hard, not to mention that crap makes you dizzy. A girl would be considered brawlic if she performs beyond the requisite slap, hair pull and windmill.

Brawlic: Referencing one's physical body, being suitable to brawl. *Ex. Christina was scared to fight Michelle because she was brawlic like a man.*

The windmill aside, a girl fight was basically a soft porn show for teen boys. I know this because I have watched many a girl fight unfold. As girls fought, people crowded around pouring out of their classrooms shouting the news and picking sides. From this melee a distinct cry erupted. Like I said, Shan don't usually get involved in no drama, but I am a teenager and this is high school, my curiosity got the best of me. If curiosity killed the cat, I edge in closer to see if satisfaction would bring him back. After a few seconds I pulled away, it just wasn't my style. I did the next best thing to being at the fight and put in a text to Corey. Corey was like a news anchor who gave blow-by-blow plays of the action. He imitated Howard Cosell, "The girls are in a state of undress, I don't know who is on which team. Ladies and gentleman, the windmills are flying and the guaranteed hair on the floor has exceeded its quota." Corey is my boy, but no doubt like every other boy, he hoped to get a peek of skin especially of a woman's bra or even better a Janet Jackson breast malfunction.

At one point I couldn't even make out what Corey was saying. I was shouting, Huh? What? Huh? Finally, I was able to decipher what the mostly male

audience was chanting, "Rip the bra, rip the bra."   I
guess this was why Corey could no longer report what
was going on. He was too busy staring.

In one of those windmill rotations, a hand must
have hooked onto a shirt and raised it above the head to
expose a bra.

Imagine my recent boob development exposed to
the public or sabotaged by a spin from the windmill. I
can't even Aw Shucks that one. I gotta say, "Oh hell no!"

Okay, back to Corey giving me the story about
the girl fight and, "Rip the bra." I have to admit I
snickered. I laughed so hard I snorted a little. That's
funny as hell. Mean, but funny nonetheless.

Romance

Believe me when I tell you I was surprised to find out that behind all that locker drama two girls were fighting over the transfer student. They did not even know his name. With hair, nails and attitudes all over the hall, the crew did a visual to check that we were all alright. Then we gave the signal to meet in our conference space.

That's not exactly how it happened, but... We had all arrived except for our newest crew member, Nia. Nia not only kept us waiting, but she had the audacity to bring old boy with her. Still none of us had learned the transfer students' name. "Everybody good?" I asked immediately, not wanting to move from Corey and especially not letting dude disrupt our flow.

Imagine, that he was the first one to speak? "I apologize for crowding your spot, but your homegirl Nia just dragged me along. I did not mean to bring no bad vibes your way." "Hold up", I shouted, "You mean to tell me all that was over you?!"

It was then that I had grabbed Corey's hand and

commanded Nikki to come on. We left Ms. Thang and dude in our conference space.

I knew Corey liked me! We were still holding hands as we reached the lobby of the school. I was feeling excited and nervous. My palms were beginning to sweat. I lay my head on Corey's shoulder and take the scent of his cologne home with me.

Corey's hand was smooth like it had been lotioned, but masculine enough to know that he was strong. It sure did feel good when he held me. I have never imagined a kiss so sweet, but the quick heat of the moment did not allow the kiss to linger.

In all of the madness of the fight, Corey had grabbed me. When he pulled me to him, our faces were so close. Without notice, he kissed me. The press of his soft firm, lips and the strength of his hand, I will never forget. This was my first real kiss.

While I am off in LaLa land, replaying the kiss that I shared with Corey, Nikki was feverishly texting on her phone. Her phone was lighting up and bleeping in response. I don't know when she found the time to take a picture of the schools' mystery man, but since Nia had dragged him into our space, all bets were off.

With a final bleep of her phone, Nikki shouted, "Check this out." The response she got on the mystery man was that his name was Malik, dka, Leek the Freak. OMG! What the kind of name is that?

DKA (n) Don Juan Known As... Similar to the female DKA, Diva Known As. *Ex. Yeah I know that dude Malik, DKA Leek the Freak.*

I was so curious about Nikki's phone activity and the news she reported that when I glanced around to survey the scene, Corey was gone. Just as quickly as Corey was by my side during the fight, he was now absent.

None of the days events such as a mystery man, friendship, the sweetest kiss, and the realization that everyone was not carrying a V-card were advertised in the high school catalog. I was not enlisted in a drama program, but... all this action required stage hands and camera crews.

If there ever was a time to say Aw Shucks, it was now.

Aw Shucks!

Glossary

 - This book icon is used to identify the definiton of a word.

Aiight(adj) - an abbreviation of alright that signals agreement or state of being good. *Ex. How you feeling? I'm aiight.*

Baller(n) - A high level of social and financial status where one was put on a pedestal and highly regarded. *Ex. By the make of his suit, I can tell that he is a baller.*

Bird(n) - A group of females that hang together. The females are characterized as loud and unsophisticated. *Ex. Please do not say anything like that again, you sound like a bird.*

Boo(n) - A romantic or physical other in someone's life. Not to be confused with boy or girlfriend. *Ex. I am so glad that my Boo asked me to the school dance.*

Brawlic(adj) - Referencing one's physical body, being suitable to brawl. *Ex. Christina was scared to fight Michelle because she was brawlic like a man.*

Bread(n) - A colloquial term meaning money. Synonyms: dough, cash, mullah, stocks, paper, guap. *Ex. She spent a lot of bread at the mall.*

DKA(n) - Diva known As
Ex. Ms. Linda dka Ms. L, is our advisory teacher.

DKA(n) - Don Juan Known As... Similar to the female DKA, Diva Known As.
Ex. Yeah I know that dude Malik, DKA Leek the Freak.

Get washed(v) - what is said about the person who loses the fight. *Ex. Yeah, Niecy had a black eye. She got washed by Cookie.*

Ghost(v) - to quickly disappear
Ex. When we heard sirens, we were ghost.

Government(n) - The name that is issued to you and noted on your birth certificate. This is the name by which the government recognizes you for tax purposes. *Ex. Yo, why are you shouting my government across the hall?*

Jump off (n) - Something that acts as a catalyst, the motivating force for subsequent events. *Ex. Thanksgiving is usually the jump off for seasonal weight gain.*

One (n) - closure. Usually a way to end a conversation, synonymous with okay, or to show unity as in one mind. *Ex. I will talk to you later, One.*

Pretty brown round (n) - A females butt! Synonyms: a phatty or cake. *Ex. That girl's pretty brown round looks proper in them jeans.*

Salty (v) - A state of being bitter.
Ex. Nikki was salty when I nodded and walked away.

Trippin(v) - Relates to the drug or situational induced state   that alters normal mental thought processes or shock. *Ex. The news about their divorce had everyone trippin.*

Tight (v) - A feeling of anger.
Ex. I know you were tight when you could not go to the dance last week.

About The Author

T. Holland is the pen name of Tanganyika Lindner. Both the writer and the woman are sassy and enjoy using words as a power tool. By spirit and training the author is a leader in education but takes the most pleasure in using her gifts to conduct training workshops for youth, families and businesses through her consulting company Motivate2Educate. She leads participants from being curious and uncertain to being fired up and focused. Her delivery is laced with humor and grounded in reality that spills into her writing. For sure you will leave her presence motivated!

STUDY GUIDE

*The novel explores many issues that young people face
every day. Whether you are an educator, a professional school
counselor, programmer or parent please know that this book is
definitely a conversation starter.*

*To assist you in directing this dialog, I offer my email address
at motivate2educate@yahoo.com You are welcome to contact
me to secure study guide material for use in classrooms and
with advisory groups. The guide is available for an additional
cost.*

*The author is also available for book chats, literary circles,
signings and guest appearances.*

*You can also contact: Power House Publication
(contactus@phmstudios.com) for more
information on the author.*

Aw Shucks!
Diary of a Little Diva by T. Holland

*Check out more in a series of books by the author and look out
for more titles from Power House Media™ Publication.
www.powerhousepublication.com*

*Coming soon from T. Holland is a novel geared more toward an
adult audience "**Just Trying to Get It**" The novel will
explore dating and living in NYC.*

POWER HOUSE MEDIA PUBLICATION

Diary of a Little Diva

Breinigsville, PA USA
03 April 2011
258997BV00005B/4/P